THE REAL DOPEBOYZ OF SOUTH CENTRAL

BARBIE SCOTT

The Real Dopeboyz of South Central

Copyright © 2018 by Barbie Scott

Published by Shan Presents
www.shanpresents.com

This is a work of fiction. Any references or similarities to actual events, real people, living or dead, or to the real locals intended to give the novel a sense of reality. Any similarity in other names, characters, places, and incidents are entirely coincidental.

Subscribe

Text Shan to 22828 to stay up to date with new releases, sneak peeks, contest, and more....

Want to be a part of Shan Presents?

To submit your manuscript to Shan Presents, please send the first three chapters and synopsis to submissions@shanpresents.com

ONE

Calhoun

_____

I bought a AP to fuck it up
I'm just tryna run the cake up
Versace sheets just to make love
Got a private just to make drugs
'Cause I'm tryna flood the face up
I been fuckin' with the same plug
I been fuckin' with these rich niggas
Had to whip it with my wrist, nigga
Then I got it on my wrist, nigga

I bobbed my head to the sounds of Roddy Ricch's *Fuck It Up* as I pulled out everything I needed to cook up my work. I pulled off my hoodie because this was gonna be a long ass night. I had to cook up four birds to distribute, so, I would be in the kitchen for at least five hours. On a regular, this was what my life consisted of. If I wasn't in the kitchen, I was at one of my traps making sure shit was running smooth. Because I didn't have a bitch; not that I wanted one, I'd spend my free time riding my dirt bike. A nigga like me didn't have much of a life. All I gave a fuck about

1

was my money. I knew sooner or later, I'd have a shorty and when that day came, I was gonna make sure his or her future was secure.

As I dropped the pot into the water, the sound of my business phone rang making me look over. When I noticed it was one of my workers, I picked it up from countertop and answered it.

"In the lab, what's up?" I told him, so he could make it quick.

"Man, it's slow as a muthafucka round here Calhoun."

"Well, nigga go find the feins."

"I have, but it's been like this the last couple weeks," he said, sounding annoyed. This nigga already knew what was up. If he didn't make his money, then that meant he wasn't making mine. And if I wasn't getting paid, then niggas was getting cut. And that's exactly how shit went.

"So, how you been turning in yo bread?"

"Shit, I been giving it to you out my stash."

"A'ight, I'mma holla at East so he can roll through and see what's up."

"A'ight man," Coogi said, disconnecting the line.

I shook my head because I couldn't understand why was this spot out of all the spots running slow. I mean damn, I had the purest dope on the streets and my only competition was my best friend who was like my brother *East*.

East and I worked together, but he pretty much ran his own spots and even cooked his own work. Because our hand game was different, that gave the fiens a different taste. Often, we would bet on who shit was the best and always, I'd win. I was the muthafucking man on these streets. I had learned how to whip my work from the Gee, homegirl, Toni, years ago. Toni was a hog when it came to cooking up. She had the smokers going bananas over her work. That chick was like the Griselda Blanco of the Eastside, so I made sure to pay close attention and perfect this shit.

Right now she was serving a eight-year bid, but from what her younger daughter told me, she had about two years left because she only had to do six years off the eight. When she touched down, I had something setup for her. I knew how shit was when a nigga went to sit down. Some people either had a stash buried or came home to nothing.

Once I perfected my hand game, I took over the streets of South Central. I was what the DA would refer to as a *Kingpin*. Not only did I have the purest white crack, but I had started dabbling in some new shit that surfaced in the urban community called Meth. Racking in at least 10 bands a day, I was content. I could have made more, but I was trying to stay off the police radar. It was two things I could be in life and that was; a killa or a hustla, but my dumbass did both. I mean, I didn't kill intentionally, but when niggas tested me, I had to get my hands dirty.

After proving a point to niggas, the entire city knew that fucking with me would have mothers crying and homies dying, so I eased up on killing. I was what most people would call *Ruthless,* but to me I was just Anthony Calhoun; a nigga that just wanted to survive South Central.

What I meant by survive, was, just because I had dough, I still couldn't stay out the hood. Shit this all I knew. I was born and raised in the trap, so I had it honest. Now, don't get shit twisted. I also knew, you couldn't shit where you lay, so of course, I had a nice ass beach house ducked off in Marina Del Rey. I also had a crib out in Westchester that I slept at occasionally. The crib in the West was mostly occupied by my little sister Marium who was now 19 and a Nana name Ella I had hired to watch over her. I had gotten custody of Mari when she was 13 years old.

My pops was heavy in the drug game, but instead of him trappin' in the hood, he went out of state to get his paper. On one of his many trips, my mother tagged along and to be honest, I couldn't even tell y'all what happened. All I knew was, they were found dead in the snow and my moms was shot so bad and burned they couldn't

ID her. My aunt Gina was more than sure it was her because who else would it have been? At this time, I was only five and Mari had just been born. We were taken into the system and not one of my family members came to get us.

As I got older, my foster parents had become pretty lenient, which was how I started hustling. I had a goal and a mission and that was to cop a crib and get my sister out the system. I stayed on corners all night to do what I had to do. I'm talking running from police and dodging jackboys. When the time came for me to be let free, my foster pops had made me some check stubs and said I worked for his business. Shit worked so I was able to use it for my crib and CPS to get Mari.

Until this day, I still took care of my foster parents. They didn't have to take me in, but they did so I had mad respect for them. Sitting back just thinking about those days always touched a soft spot for me. I missed my mom and dad like a muthafucka all though I was too young to remember them. I guess it was just the thought of having my biological parents is what I missed.

At twenty-four years old, I was doing pretty good for myself. I had the city on lock with the dope and I was the most feared nigga in the hood. Everybody said I was a split image of my father because everybody around the way knew who Big Calhoun was. I hated that I adapted his name, but because it was our last name, it stuck.

I went by the name Cali, so I could be different from my pops. Standing at 6'2 and weighing 250 pounds, my complexion I got from my mother for sure. I had brown skin and deep waves. A nigga was blessed with a dimple, but that was only for me because I really didn't give a fuck about the compliments I received from the women. With me, these chicks were a fuck and go thing. The only three women I loved were my little sister, my foster mother, and my aunt Rene who found my sister and I a couple years ago.

My aunt Rene was another story for another time, but just know, I love that lady like a muthafucka. I mean, how could I not, she was blood. Aunt Gina had pretty much said fuck us and because of that, I turned the other cheek to her bitch ass whenever she called for something. Aunt Rene was my pops sister and Gina was my mom's sibling.

The sound of my phone ringing brought me back from relishing in my past. A nigga was in a straight zone. The water literally boiled all out the pot. I grabbed my phone and put it to my ear as I added more water into the pot.

"Fuck you want hoe?" I playfully said to my nigga East.

"Say bitch we got a problem," he said, sounding stressed out.

East was the only nigga that could get away with that bitch word because how close we were. One of my other homies tried to pull that shit with me and ended up in the dumpster in the alley on King Blvd. I didn't play with these niggas and I wasn't gonna start now.

See, East and I were more than homies. That nigga was my brother from another mother. We had grown up together, but when I got taken away, we lost contact. The day we ran into each other, a nigga was damn near ready to tear up like a hoe. East was all I had from my childhood memories, so the moment was sentimental for a nigga. If I didn't remember shit else, I remembered East. I mean shit we were inseparable. I really didn't have nobody but him because my moms and dad stayed busy. I swear I'd go to bat over this nigga and it was vice versa.

"Talk to me hoe, I'm in the kitchen."

"Cooking up that nasty shit. Gone kill somebody one day," we laughed.

"Man, fuck you. My shit better than yours," we joked.

"Ayo, so the nigga Coogi called me and told me what was up. I slid through there and hollered at a couple feins and they say some nigga name Dee round our section serving."

"Fuck you mean?"

"Nigga, what I said."

"So, who is this nigga?"

"Nigga, yo guess is as good as mine. But they say they ain't see him."

"Who ain't seen him?"

5

"The smokers. It's like this nigga a fucking ghost."

"Yeah a'ight. I'mma slide through."

"A'ight hit me."

"One." I hung up the phone mad as fuck.

Right now, I had to focus on my work, but when I was done, I was gonna go investigate this shit. Niggas knew not to play with me. I didn't step on nobody toes when I opened up shops. The parts of town I fucked with was neutral and I made sure to open up my traps far from other niggas' traps. As for my dope taking over the game, that wasn't my fault.

Pulling up around the corner from my trap, I jumped out the car like a mad man. All eyes were on me and niggas looked scared to death. I wiped out my strap and walked up on the crowd of niggas that were chilling on a fire hydrant. A few niggas scattered and the niggas that stayed around immediately started questioning my actions.

"Man, Cali what's up?" one nigga name OJ asked.

OJ was the only nigga on this side I respected. See right here on this block these niggas sold weed, which was why I came here. OJ was the one who had the sack and the nigga they all answered to.

"Who the fuck is Dee, OJ?"

"I don't know my nigga. Put that strap up please man," he said, looking down at my gun.

"I ain't putting shit up because niggas is testing me. I'm hearing somebody short stopping my spot and the nigga name is Dee."

"On my kids, I don't know a Dee and all we pushing is trees," he said, and I could tell he was shook up. I hated I had to come at OJ like this, but these niggas knew not to play with me.

"Yeah a'ight. I'mma hold you to it my nigga." I shot him a look that told him I wasn't playing.

I jumped in my whip and went to the other side where there were always tents full of smokers. Shit looked and smelled like death, but this was our environment. I jumped out my car and before I could get up on the tent, about ten smokers rushed me asking for a hit.

"Kojak, come here." I ordered.

Kojak was that one smoker everybody had in the hood that stole any and everything you wanted. He fucked all the smoker chicks and even called himself Fresh. Nigga thought he was still young and hip, but he was gone off crack and had been gone for years.

"Cali, what's up baby you got something for me to do? Nigga need some of that booyah," he said, referring to my work.

"Yeah, I do got some work for you." I told him and pulled him to the side. I explained what I needed him to do and he took off in full speed.

I pulled up the street from the house and watched as Kojak walked up to the old worn down home. It was like twenty seconds max and the nigga was walking over to my whip. He bent over into the window and held out his hand for me to see. Sure enough, he had a fat ass rock in his hand. Clenching my jaw, I was ready to go into the spot dumping. The way I was feeling, I didn't give a fuck who was inside.

"So, was it Dee?" I asked him, but looking towards the home.

"I don't know man. They don't let you in. They serve you through a makeshift little glass window."

Instead of responding, I nodded my head. "Aight good looking," I told him, then rolled my window up. I didn't have to pay the nigga because he had just copped a fat ass fifty piece from the house.

"It's a green light on the crib," I told East as soon as he answered.

"What you plan on doing?"

"Watch this muthafucka for a couple days until I see movement."

"A'ight, a'ight, so what you bout to get into?"

"Shit, some pussy the way I'm feeling."

"Nasty ass nigga," he said and we both laughed.

"Shut yo ol in love ass up bitch," I said and hung his ass up.

I dialed Jazzy's number and because I already knew she was gonna say yes, I headed in the direction of her home. I was gonna call it a night because I was back on this Dee nigga first thing in the morning.

TWO

East

$\mathscr{P}$ulling up to Griffith Ave., I hopped out my car to run into the store to grab some Backwoods. I said my what's up to the few niggas that hung in front the store, then made my way in. I walked straight to the counter and purchased my blunts, then headed back out the door. I drove a few blocks down to the trap that I ran, but I sat in the car to observe my surroundings. One thing about me, is I always moved with caution. I wasn't like Cali by far. That nigga was wild and moved loosely. I was the brother with the brains and what a nigga like him needed on his team. I had a couple years on Cali, so I was like the big brother to my friend. I had to give it to my mans, that nigga had put me on when I was at my lowest. I swear it was like fate running into him after all these years.

When Cali up and disappeared, I never knew he was taken away. I thought they had just moved with no trace. We were young as fuck at this time. The minute I hit thirteen, I started selling dope. My moms had found out and of course, she kicked me out. I didn't have shit but a cell phone and 7 grams of dope to my name. To this day, I still held a grudge with my moms. All she gave a fuck about was my little brother. I was sleeping in smokers' houses and even in a car that I had finally been able to cop. You think she gave a fuck? Hell nah. It was fuck me and until this day, the feelings were mutual.

Cali and I were like two peas in a pod. Only difference was our looks and I had a fiancé. Cali on the other hand was single and a bitch wasn't nowhere in his plans. I had been with Jennifer since we were younger and a year ago, I proposed. I loved Jennifer like a muthafucka because she had held me down when I didn't have shit up until I came up with Cali. When I was younger, I was on some frivolous shit in my relationship. I fucked all types of bitches and brought the drama home. On many occasions, she threatened to leave until I got my act right. Realizing I was on the verge of really losing her, I got my shit together and we been good ever since.

The sound of arguing broke me out my daze. I looked towards the trap and noticed Jock, one of my workers, arguing with a chick I'd never seen. She didn't look like a smoker so I assumed it was one of his bitches. Granted that was his business, but I didn't play that shit at my traps. I hopped out my whip and made my way towards the two. Jock threw his hands up like he was surrendering as ol girl went in on him.

"I don't give a fuck who you are when you see her don't fucking sell her any drugs!" the chick was shouting.

"Man, tell that bitch stay from around her then!" Jock yelled.

"Bitch? Nigga, I got yo bitch!" she tried to attack my nigga. I quickly grabbed her because I knew Jock like a book and beating a bitch up was a normal for him.

"Come on shawty, what's the problem?"

"Who the fuck are you?" she turned around and mugged me.

"Man, this bitch betta get away from here," Jock said adding fuel to the fire.

"Shawty, shawty come on. Trust me this ain't what you want." I told her in my most calmest voice.

"Nigga, I ain't scared of you pussy ass niggas," she said, and I was five seconds from letting Jock beat her ass.

I wasn't no woman beater, but if I let Jock at her, she would be laid the fuck out. I couldn't have that because it was something about her that peaked my interest. Everybody in the entire community knew of me. Just because I was a laid back nigga, muthafuckas still knew not to test my gangsta. Apparently, this chick didn't know who I was and if she kept popping off she was gonna find out.

"Check it out, Lil Mama. This my city and what the fuck I say goes. I'm talking to you with manners now I expect the same respect. If you wanna get buck, I suggest you go get yo best nigga and bring him to me because I don't hit women." I told her in my most serious voice. She looked from Jock to me still wearing a mug, but she didn't say shit.

"Look," she said in a more calmer voice. "My mother came down here and bought some work. All I ask is can y'all please stop selling to her."

"And who is your mother?"

"Smoker Pearl, crack head ass." Jock said, and baby girl spent on her heels so fast.

"Man, go the fuck in the house." I told him.

"Man, why the fuck..."

"Nigga, so you ain't gone listen?" I stepped up closer to him.

He could show out if he wanted to in front this chick, but Jock knew what it was. Keep it real the nigga was already on the verge of losing his job because he was slipping.

Without another word, he walked off pouting like a little bitch. I ignored the nigga then focused my attention back on ol girl.

"Now baby girl.."

"It's Kaloni," she corrected me." I swear her little slick ass mouth was kinda cute. I don't know why, but I wanted her in the worst way. I wanted her just because I wanted to tame her little ass and give her some act right. She was cute as fuck, little and petite like I liked. She had a pretty light brown complexion and a pair of slanted eyes like she was mixed.

"Kaloni, I'll holla at my niggas and make sure nobody serve yo moms. I'll also holla at my niggas in my other traps, but only on one condition."

"And what's that?" She put her hands on her hips.

"You slide me yo' number and let me tame that pussy. It seems like that's what you need," I told her all in her personal space. She tried her hardest not to look at me, but I could tell her little ass was contemplating my request.

"You promise?"

"Hell, yeah I promise. I'mma put a hurting on that thang."

"About my mama nigga," she responded, fake annoyed.

I chuckled a little and when she smiled, that lightened the mood. I handed her my phone and waited for her to put her number inside of it. After she was done, I was surprised she didn't run off. We actually stood there for another thirty minutes chopping it up. Just from her conversation, I could tell I'd like her little ass. I had her blushing and apparently, she was feeling a nigga because she hadn't left. I was gonna give miss Kaloni a call and hopefully put a hurting on her little pussy; like I said. However, I prayed she wouldn't get attached because I was already spoken for.

Kaloni

I laid in my bed for the last two days thinking about Mr. East. The nigga hadn't called like he promised, but he did keep his word about my feeding my mother's drug habit. She came into the house cursing me out saying that none of the traps wouldn't help her craving and apparently, someone told her it was her daughter because she came in fussing. Instead of her understanding I was doing this for her own good, she called me all kinds of bitches and told me go to hell. Little did she know, I was already living in hell. I had a crack head for a mother, an unknown trick daddy of a father and I worked at Walgreens, which was the crappiest job ever because I didn't get paid enough to deal with all them different attitudes. I lived in the hood, but I tried my hardest not to let it break me. I tried my best not to be seen or know any neighbors out of embarrassment.

Just two years ago, you couldn't tell me this would be my life. I mean I was one of those starved child's, but I was deprived my childhood. I had to basically take care of my mother, which consisted of paying the rent, buying food and paying all the bills. We had lucked up on a low-income building after waiting over a year for our name to be called. The once nice neighborhood we lived in, in Torrance was a major change. The moment we moved here, everything took a turn for the worst. My mom couldn't afford our old home, so we moved out. We weren't here a good six months and already she was using.

Back in the days, I'd heard the stories of her abusing drugs and prostitution from my family. Because it was so many years later, I didn't expect her to go down that road again. She was doing good for herself and held a pretty good job as a medical biller from home. This time it's like the drugs took over her and she had given up on me and life. If you asked me, the abuse started before we moved, which is why we had to move.

All I had in this world was my best friend Dreu. She was my backbone and I owed her my life. Many of times I came up short on rent and she would help me out. A lot of times, I would deny being short because I was too damn prideful to admit it, but she knew me like a book and would insist. When I needed advice on men, she was my go to. When I lost my virginity, she was right by my side. Dreu and I had been friends for years. She's the reason we found the low-income building because she lived nearby with her grandma.

She called me one day and told me they had a sign up that said *Accepting Applications*, so I came to put my mother's name on the list. Dreu was a hustla, but she made sure to keep me out of harm's way. We would chill all the time, but she we would always depart ways because she had to make her money. When I say that girl was much stronger than me, I meant it. She walked around every day like she didn't have a care in the world when in fact, we had similar situations.

Her mother died years ago from a drug overdose and just like me, she was fatherless. Her grandma raised her and her little brother Micah. Micah was now eleven and Dreu did a great job at helping her grandma raise him. He was a straight A student and just like me, she kept him out the streets.

"Bestfriendddd!" I heard Dreu's voice from outside of my bedroom window.

I lifted from the bed with a smile plastered on my face because I hadn't seen her in three days. Normally, her ass would stop by my job, but she had been MIA.

"Come outside hoe," she said, smiling from ear to ear.

"Let me put my shoes on." I ran from the window and slid into my Nike slides.

When I made it downstairs, Dreu was busy on her phone. Because she told me come outside, I knew she wanted to go to the store, then maybe sit on her granny's porch and chill like we did on a regular.

"You mean to tell me you ain't hustling." I used my hands to add quotation marks.

"Nah, shit kinda weird around there," she said but didn't go into details. Like I said, she kept me out of that part of her life, so I didn't bother to ask what she meant. "Anyway, I missed yo weird ass," she laughed and playfully hit me.

"Awe I missed you, too. I knew you were busy, so I didn't want to bother you."

"So, what you been doing? Cooped up in that damn room," she answered her own question.

"Pretty much, shit. I was off work yesterday and today, so I just been chilling. Micah and I went to the park yesterday."

"Awe thank you," she squealed, but she knew she didn't have to thank me. I loved that little boy like he was my little brother.

"You know it's cool, Dreu. I love that kid," I told her and meant it.

See Dreu and I had that type of relationship. Her granny would call me to run errands for her and even Micah would call when he wanted to go to the park or needed help with his homework. Dreu's granny didn't sweat the fact she was never home because she did a lot around the house financially.

"I'mma take my ass home today," she said and looked off into the sky.

I wanted so bad to ask her what was wrong because she had this worried look. Like I said before, she was so strong nothing bothered her. And if it did, no one would ever know. I tried over and over to tell her I was here for her if she needed to talk, but she would never open up.

"Good, you need to go home," I told her, and she smirked at me.

"A'ight Granny," she said and laughed.

She always called me that when I tried to tell her something for her own good. And not only that, but, she said I lived like a granny.

As soon as we walked out the liquor store, a CLS 550 pulled up into the parking lot. I knew it could only have been a Dope Boy because Doctors and Lawyers sure in the hell didn't drive around this part of town. Dreu and I continued to walk unfazed by whoever was in the car and suddenly, I heard my name being called. I tried to ignore him as my heart fluttered. I knew exactly who that voice belonged to, but I was upset at him because he never called.

"Kaloni, I know yo ass hear me ma," the voice got closer, which told me he was now out the car. I turned around and put my hands on my hips to let him know I had an attitude.

"Let me find out," I heard Dreu mumble as she stopped with me.

"Girl, he ain't nobody," I told her, but making sure he heard me.

"Oh, I ain't nobody?" he laughed, but I didn't see shit funny. "She lying like a muthafucka'. I'm her future husband." He wrapped his arms around me.

"Well, I know that's a lie." Dreu rolled her eyes.

"What you mean?" he asked her.

"Nigga, because that's my best friend and trust me if y'all were even that close, I would have been the one to approve you."

"Damn, it's like that?" East looked from Dreu to me. I smirked my lips and titled my head.

"Come on nigga! We ain't got time for no bitches right now." Whoever the nigga was with East said, as he walked out the store.

Oh shit. I thought because he picked the wrong bitches today. Dreu didn't have no filter and I knew she was about to go up.

"Nigga, I got yo bitch!" she said and went to reach in her pocket. I quickly grabbed her arm and pulled her away.

"Please no, Dreu," I pleaded in her ear, nervously.

"What the fuck you thought you was about to do?" the guy said as he made his way to us.

"Get yo homie, East," I told him and pulled Dreu away.

"Chill nigga," I heard him telling his rude ass friend. "I'mma call you," he said and turned to head for his car. *That was a close one*; I thought because shit was gonna get ugly.

As Dreu and I walked towards her grandmother's house, she was quiet, and I hated when she got like that. I knew she was upset, so I tried to lighten the mood.

"I be glad when my car get fixed. Bitch can't be walking in this heat."

"Who was that nigga, Kaloni?" she said, ignoring me. I sighed before I answered.

"This guy I met the other day."

"Well, you need to stay away from him," she said like she was my mother. Dreu was hella over protective of me and that's another thing that drove me crazy.

"He cool, Dreu"

"Nah, he ain't cool. Nine out of ten he's a heartbreaking ass D boy that only wanna fuck you. Nigga prolly got all kinds of bitches stashed away with babies running around and shit. How the fuck you meet him anyway?" She stopped walking and looked at me.

"To be honest, it was crazy," I told her.

She looked at me as if she wasn't letting up, so I began telling her about the day I met him. I knew she wasn't gonna approve, but because he had granted my wishes, he was already a plus in my book. I failed to mention to her that I stayed and talked to him for a while and I was actually digging him. I mean he didn't have to do that for me and not to mention, he was fine as hell.

East had a really cute face and his tapered cut only added to his sexy structure. He was kinda big like I liked them. Not fat or anything, just big like he had spent many days and nights in the gym. This was my second time seeing him and like the first time, he was dressed niced. He wasn't all extra flashy. He wore a nice chain and a simple watch that I was sure cost a lot. Unlike the guy that was with him. That nigga had on three chains, a huge pair of earrings, and a bracelet that held so many diamonds it sparkled in the sun. Like I said, I knew Dreu wouldn't approve, but I was grown, and I was anticipating his call.

THREE

Dreu
___

For a couple days, I laid low because I heard niggas was watching my spot. I couldn't understand why because I minded my business and didn't bother nobody. But that's what came with California. Niggas hated seeing the next muthafucka eat. One thing about me though is I always made sure to move with caution. I didn't have a team of killas behind me. It was just me and my loyal crack heads. For a couple rocks, they kept me on my toes about things.

Years ago, I had met a smoker thru Kaloni's mom name Brenda. Brenda was one of those clean smokers that kept herself up. She let me serve out her home as long as I fed her habit and helped with the light bill. She ended up being really sweet and her husband Charles was cool, too. Charles also abused drugs and he looked like he was on his last limb. He was really old, and crack had taken a toll on his life. He always stayed inside the room in his bed watching television.

"So, what did you think about his friend?" Kaloni asked, bringing me back on track. I knew why she asked, but that shit wasn't gonna work.

"That nigga ugly as fuck," I lied.

I knew what she was trying to do and I wasn't falling for it. I wasn't pressed for no nigga right now because I was focused on my money. Niggas were problems and as fine as that nigga was, I knew drama came with his ass. I wished Kaloni would listen to me and fall back off East because just like the other nigga, he looked like drama. I've told Kaloni over and over that a Dope Boy wasn't for her, but that's all her ass was attracted to. She thought I was dumb. She thought I didn't know she liked East, but I knew her all too well. The way she looked at that nigga was like the way Nicki looked at Meek when they were on stage.

"Let's go to Club Savage tonight?" I tried to change the subject.

"Bitch. you know I don't wanna club."

"That's what's wrong with you, Granny. Yo' ass always working or cooped up in this damn house. Damn I ain't seen you in days." I playfully rolled my eyes. I was hoping she said yes because I needed to get out bad. I had been cooped up in my trap five straight days. I was ready to shake some ass.

"Okaaaay damn," she said, agreeing to come along.

"Okay, I'mma hit Pookie and let him know we coming."

Pulling out my phone, I went to my Instagram and typed in @kingofturnuppookiefnrude. Pookie F'n Rude was the hottest promoter in Cali. I had met him years ago at a club called Barbies Palace and we had been cool since then. I sent him the message then focused my attention back to Kaloni. I knew she was about to stress over something to wear because she was going through her drawers, then slamming them shut. I stood up and walked to my closet. I spotted a cute little black dress that still had a tag on it.

"Wear this, it's cute."

"This is cute." She grabbed it and started examining it. "So, what you wearing? I mean this dress is brand new, Dreu"

"I don't know yet, but it's cool ma."

"Thank you," she smiled excited.

"Dreu! That damn boy done called six times," my grandma, said busting into the room.

I rolled my eyes, but not at her. I was about tired of this nigga Kendall. He was a real fucking bugaboo. Kendall and I had messed around for a year until I dumped his ass. He was actually the one that took my virginity and I regretted it. First of all, I thought my first time would be magical; but hell nah. Nigga was twenty and didn't know what he was doing. He had no stroke and he nutted before I could even get over the pain.

I had sex with him a few times after and every time, it was the same shit. I only strung him along because he treated me good. Actually, a little too good that it was kind of corny. Like he was too damn submissive to me no matter how rude I treated him. I was hoping he would leave me alone, but that shit didn't work. I stopped messing with him about three months ago and this nigga called every day. I told him over and over I didn't want a relationship, but he wouldn't let up.

"Ugh, I'm so glad I stopped fucking with Mark," Kaloni said, laughing.

Mark was Kendall's friend that she messed with for five months. We actually lost our virginity together. Same house, different rooms with two best friends. When she first met him, she liked him a lot, but the nigga was a straight hoe. When I say, I had to beat up at least four bitches in that little time, I kid you not. I didn't play when it came to my best friend, so I always fought her battles. Kaloni was the more reserved one of us.

"Tell him I moved, Grandma." She rolled her eyes.

Kaloni and I fell out laughing, which annoyed my Grandma more. She pulled the door closed and went to her usual seat, which was in the kitchen. I don't know why, but my granny sat at the kitchen table and read all day. I loved that lady to death and if something ever happened to her, I would die.

My Grandma Ella Mae had raised me. My mother had passed when I was a little girl from a drug overdose. I'm not gonna sit here and discredit my moms because her addiction. She was the best in my eyes. I wasn't no fool, I knew my mom did drugs because as a child I was very observant. However, she took good care of me and whenever she was in my presence, I lit up like Christmas lights. Now as far as my dad went, I had no idea who he was and really didn't care. Can't miss what I never had right?

At a young age, I watched the way my moms moved. Seeing her fall victim to drugs, I told myself I'd be the muthafucka on the opposite side. I mean shit it killed my mother, so why have remorse for anyone else. The only person I didn't serve was Ms. Pearl. That was Kaloni's mom and I respected my friend enough to not do it. Recently, Ms. Pearl came crying at my spot saying no one around would serve her and I guess that's where East came in at. Kaloni had told me the entire story about the day she went flexing at his trap house. That was the only thing I gave him. He didn't have to do that and he did, so I'd give him that. No matter how cool he was, I was gonna do everything in my power to keep her from messing with him.

~

Club Savage

Walking into Club Savage, the entire club was packed and everyone was partying. This is what I liked about this club. Everyone was always in tune with each other and living their best life. The DJ here was pretty dope and they always went live with *The Real Cousins.* The Real Cousins were two chicks that had a cyber radio station. They did major interviews and had some of the hottest guest on their show. Their Duo consists of two chicks named Aja and Britney and a DJ named DJ Deezy I had met them a couple times on the club scene.

Walking through the crowd, we made our way to our table. Because I had ran into Pookie at the door, he had security bring us up to a VIP table that I requested would be in the cut. I loved the low-key tables because I could smoke my weed and hide from the locals. I was sorta anti. Okay I was hella anti. I didn't mingle much with strangers and I really didn't fuck with many people in my city. I wasn't a people person at all. I don't know why, I guess it was because for many years, I was a loner. And to this day, I'm still a loner. The only friend I have is Kaloni and that's how it would always be.

As soon as I sat down, I took my jean jacket off and got comfy in my seat. As we waited for our bottle of Hennessy, we began to chat about the crowd. They were partying hard. I couldn't wait to get drunk and shake my ass. Suddenly, the DJ switched to Big Bank YG. I couldn't even hold it anymore, I jumped up and started popping my ass. Kaloni was laughing at me with her granny ass. I knew as soon as she got drunk enough, she'd be joining me.

"Ugh, you invited him?" I said, looking over at Loni.

She reluctantly looked up. I rolled my eyes at her in disgust. I was really disgusted when I saw his rude ass homeboy behind him. He looked annoyed just as I was. He had a cup in his hand and in the other he was holding a champagne bottle.

"We got Calhoun and East in the building. I see you my niggas," the DJ said over the mic.

Calhoun as I now knew, raised his glass then began bobbing his head. I wanted so bad to sit down, but I couldn't because Nicki part had just begun to play. I pretended like they weren't here and kept dancing. East sat beside Kaloni and his boy stood beside them. *Damn he fine as fuck.* I thought annoyed with my thoughts. I couldn't front, this nigga wasn't only fine as fuck, his ass dressed nice and his jewelry had him looking like one of those rich ass rappers.

"What's up, Dreu?" East said, smirking.

I rolled my eyes at his ass because the nigga didn't even know me. *Saying my name like we good or some shit.*

"Stuck up ass," Calhoun said, then took a sip of his drink.

I didn't bother to respond because this nigga wasn't worth my time.

"I'll be back, I gotta pee," I told Kaloni.

I lied like a muthafucka. I needed to get away from Calhoun and fast. This nigga had my panties soaking wet. Just thoughts of what

I'll do to him, had me mad. I wasn't supposed to be having these thoughts, but I was, and I couldn't help it.

As I walked away, I could feel him watching my ass. I turned around and our eyes met. It's like he was speaking to me with his eyes, but that was a front. That nigga was a complete asshole just like me. I quickly turned from him and walked towards the ladies' room. As soon as I made it inside, I used the restroom then walked over to wash my hands.

"Wait, aren't you the girl with Calhoun and East?" some girl asked the minute she walked into the bathroom.

"I ain't with them niggas," I responded, smartly.

"Oh, okay. I saw you in their VIP. Well, can me and my friend come up please? I been trying to get that nigga for years."

"I don't give a fuck. He ain't my man," I shrugged.

I wanted so bad to tell her thirsty ass no, but fuck it, I was in a good mood and I needed the laugh anyway.

"Ohhh, thank you," her friend said, smiling from ear to ear.

I snatched up a paper towel and dried my hands off. I turned to walk out the door, but the door came crashing in. Calhoun barged in and walked up on me.

"What's up with yo stuck up ass shorty you need some dick," he told me more so than asking.

The scent of his cologne mixed with weed had me ready to drop my panties right here in this bathroom. *Lord he just caused a waterfall in my draws;* I thought ready to scream. *Play it cool Dreu, play it cool;* I coached myself.

"I get enough dick. Fuck I need yours for?" I spat matching his tone. "Oh, and baby girl right here checking for you. She might want that contaminated shit," I told him, then walked out. The two chicks stood looking priceless. I know they were confused, but it didn't matter. Whether we were fucking or not, she was still gonna fuck him.

I walked out the restroom and headed back over to my table. The bucket was sitting there with the bottle along with two more bottles that I assumed East and Calhoun ordered. I poured my glass then took a seat. I watched the aisle way on the low. I was waiting on this nigga to come back over and just the thought of him with them bitches, had me kinda jealous. I took a big gulp of my drink, followed by another. I was trying to get faded tonight and hopefully block out my thoughts of this nigga.

An entire hour went by and I was good and drunk. I was lowkey in my feelings because this nigga Calhoun still hadn't came back. I was thinking all types of shit, which was pissing me off more. When he finally came, he still had the two chicks with him. When they walked over to our table, the one chick was smiling at me trying to be nice, but I wasn't feeling friendly right now. Like always, I rolled my eyes at the bitch and stood up. Kaloni was busy entertaining her boo, so I walked downstairs to the dance floor. I was about to do something out the normal; I was gonna back my thang up on one of these niggas.

I waited for the right song and when I heard Tyga's *Taste*, I smiled because this was the perfect song. I walked to the middle of the floor and began dancing by myself. I tried my hardest to hold my dress down because it kept rising. Before I knew it, some nigga got behind me, and I couldn't front, the nigga was keeping up. I popped my ass with my hands in the air. I turned around and did a sexy little smirk. The guy I was dancing with wasn't cute at all, but he was dressed nice and smelled good. We playfully flirted as I kept dancing. I looked up because I could feel someone watching me.

Calhoun was eyeing me as he drank from his bottle. He didn't look too pleased with what went on with me and old boy and I got a kick out of it. I turned from Calhoun and focused back on my dance. I couldn't get Calhoun off my mind for shit. We danced for another two songs before I was ready to curve his ass.

"Come here," I heard a voice that made me turn around like an obedient child.

Calhoun stood there like he was that nigga. Ol boy I was dancing with looked on as I submissively went to Calhoun. I knew how shit could turn out and I wasn't trying to be in no shoot out today.

"The fuck you want? Nigga don't come down here stunting on me like I'm yo bitch." I walked up into his space.

"Trust me, if I wanted you to be my bitch, you would. I'm just tripping off how the fuck you act so stuck up with me then down here shaking yo ass for some creep ass nigga."

"Why you worried about it? You ain't my nigga and last I checked, yo little friend up there was your concern. So, don't come checking for me."

"You know you got a smart-ass little mouth."

"Heyyy, Calhoun," some girl walked by and flirted.

The nerve of this bitch. I could have been his wife. When he looked down at her ass, I shook my head. She did have cakes for days and the small pink dress she was wearing didn't hide it.

"Exactly!" I shot at Calhoun then stormed off.

This nigga had me fucked up. Who the fuck he thought he was? He was checking for me like he knew me and I didn't know shit about him, but his name; thanks to the DJ. I hated how he got so much attention from the ladies and that's why I knew I couldn't fuck with a nigga like him. Bitches flocked to him like a bee to honey. This nigga was a real fucking Boss in the city and that shit pissed me off more.

FOUR

Calhoun

I don't know what was up with this chick, but she had a nigga intrigued. I wasn't used to no bitch dissing me and I don't know why, but she had me wanting to prove myself. I wanted to prove to her that I was that nigga. I loved a challenge and I seen already her pretty ass was gonna give me just that. I didn't even know her name, but she was my type of chick. I don't know what was little mama story, but I really didn't give a fuck. I wanted to shove this dick up in her then diss her ass since she wanted to play tough. I could tell that's all she needed to get some act right. So, guess what I was gonna do? Fuck her whole life up.

As I walked back over to the VIP, I hollered at East, so we could roll. He was caked the fuck up with ol girl with his sprung ass. I couldn't do shit but shake my head because the nigga didn't even hit the pussy and already he was acting in love. She was pretty as a mutha-fucka, but it surprised me he was even cheating. For the last couple years, the nigga had been doing good dodging bitches. Him and Jenny were in a good space finally, so it had to be something about ol girl he really liked. I couldn't get the nigga to cheat for shit on many occasions and trust me I tried. I wasn't no fucked up nigga; I just didn't believe in love and I for sure didn't trust bitches. Her little corny ass was prolly an undercover hoe, which wouldn't surprise me because all these bitches was selling pussy these days.

After ol girl said her name a few times, I had a name to go with the face. *Dreu;* I mumbled to myself. The name fit her perfectly. Dreu sat there unmoved by me, but I didn't have time for her shit tonight. I had two bitches on my arm and by the way they were acting, they both wanted to fuck a nigga.

"I'm not going nowhere with him!" I heard Dreu yell, which made me frown at her.

I didn't ask the bitch to go nowhere, so all that extra shit wasn't caused for.

"Bitch I didn..." I had to catch myself. Again, she was starting to piss me off, but I wasn't gonna let the bitch take my energy.

"Come on, Dreu, we're going to eat, then get dropped off," Kaloni told her, standing to her feet.

Dreu reluctantly got up, so I turned to walk off. East could stay with them bitches if he wanted to. See this was the reason I always tell him drive his own car.

When we walked out to the Escalade, I motioned for the driver to make a U Turn. When he pulled alongside of us, Dreu said some smart shit under her breath then lifted the seat to climb in the back. When she stood there holding the seat, I was puzzled.

"Thing 1 and Thing 2, y'all getting in the way back," she said, smartly to the two chicks.

I couldn't help but chuckle. This girl was something else. Thing 1 and Thing 2 hopped in unfazed by Dreu's rudeness. East and his Boo climbed into the third-row seat so that meant I had to ride alongside with rude ass. I walked around to the other side and hopped in. I instructed the driver to take us out to Jerry's Deli in the Marina.

As we drove, I could tell everyone was intoxicated. Thing 1 and Thing 2 were in the back laughing and entertaining each other and

East and Kaloni were indulged in their own conversation. Meanwhile, I sat in the front with the Grinch who was busy on her phone. I pulled out my phone and got lost into my messages. Every now and then, I would sneak a peek over at Dreu's thighs. Her ass was thick as a muthafucka. I couldn't front if I wanted to. She was the baddest chick in LA. She had a pretty ass face with a mole above her pouty lips. She had light brown eyes that's matched her pretty brown skin perfectly. I don't know if her hair was real or not, but it didn't matter. I liked long hair, so a weave didn't bother me.

She was so busy in her phone a nigga kinda felt jealous. She was really ignoring me like I didn't exist, which was fucking me up more. Baby girl was in the presence of a king and she wasn't fazed. I was hoping the two chicks I brought along would change her mind, but that shit didn't work.

I reached over and snatched Dreu's phone smooth out her hand. She looked at me like I lost my mind. I stuck the phone into my pocket and before I knew it, she had lunged at me like she had lost her fucking mind.

"Javier, pull over!" I told the driver. When he pulled over, I looked over at Dreu.

"Get the fuck out."

"Give my phone and I will. You think I give a fuck about getting out," she shot thinking, I was kicking her out. But little did she know we were about to duke it out.

I climbed out right behind her and waltzed over to her side of the whip.

"Come on, Billy Bad Ass, you wanna fight niggas like you tough, come on let's fight," I told her and threw my hands up in a fighting stance.

At first, she looked confused, but then, she really got into the street and matched my stance. I reached out and smacked her ass. Before I knew it, she punched me. Her little ass hit hard, but I shook that shit off. I reached out and slapped her again. Although I had my fist up, I was hitting her with open hand. We went at it for some time, until I noticed she wasn't gonna back down. I wrapped my arms around her neck and began choking her ass.

"East, he's gonna kill her," I heard Kaloni whining from the sideline.

"Man, he ain't gonna kill that girl," East responded.

"When we get back in this car, you gonna act like you got some fucking sense. You not getting this fucking phone back until you out my presence. And if you ever think about putting yo fucking hands on me again, I'mma show you why they call me Calhoun," I said into her ear.

I finally let her go and she began gasping for air. When she finally came up, she looked at me like she hated my guts.

"Fuck you!" she said, then walked over to the truck and climbed in.

I couldn't do shit but laugh because this girl was really something else. Nobody in my city talked to me like this. I was feared on these streets by men and women, but her, she didn't give a fuck and that shit was turning me on more.

When we pulled up to the restaurant, we headed in and was seated. Dreu's stubborn ass took a seat across from us and that shit pissed me off. *This bitch really testing me.* I thought eyeing her ass with so much annoyance. She tried so hard to keep from looking at me.

"Dreu, get the fuck over here." I spoke without lookin up at her. I was looking at my menu because I was gonna order even if no one else was ready. "If I gotta come get you, I'mma beat yo ass in front of all these people." This was my last and final warning. I knew she would fight me back, but she wasn't no threat. I would beat the fuck out of this girl with one hand tied behind my back.

Still focusing on my menu, I heard lips smacking, then the sound of the chair being pulled out. I knew it was her by the smell of her perfume. Not to mention, the two chicks sat across from me smacking their lips.

"What you gone get?" I leaned over to ask Dreu.

"I'm not hungry," she said, still with an attitude but I didn't give a fuck. Her ass could starve.

"Y'all know what y'all want?" I looked over at the two chicks and asked. Dreu smacked her lips, but I ignored her.

"Are y'all fucking or not?" Thing 2 asked looking from Dreu to me. I didn't need to answer because I knew Dreu was gonna answer for us.

"Bitch, don't worry about it."

"Dreu chill," Kaloni said looking scared.

"I'm not gone be too many more of your bitches. I don't know who the fuck...."

Before she could finish, Dreu had dove across the table, slamming into the chick. I sat back and let they ass fight. This bitch didn't have a place in questioning shit about me and Dreu. To be honest, her friend was the one riding my dick.

When I noticed Thing 1 jump up like she was gonna jump in, I looked over at Kaloni to see was she gonna help her friend. When I noticed she wasn't, I jumped to my feet and pulled Dreu off the girl. I mugged the other bitch as I carried her out. I wasn't into hitting bitches, but I would have punched the shit out ol girl if she attempted to hit my future wife. You damn right, I said it. This was gonna be my bitch and maybe even my wife. Dreu was a little rough around the edges, but I liked how she moved. She didn't back down for shit. I was gonna have to show her who Daddy was, but other than that, I liked her get down.

"Get the fuck off me, Calhoun. You shouldn't have brought them ditsy bitches anyway," she was shouting upset.

"Man, calm the fuck down before these people call the fucking police."

"Let's roll," East said, coming out the restaurant with Kaloni by his side.

We rushed over to the car and climbed inside leaving Thing 1 and Thing 2 behind. *Fuck them bitches*; I thought as the car pulled off.

"Where to Cali?" the driver asked.

"The beach house," I told him, referring to my crib, which was about ten minutes away. I looked over at Dreu and to my surprise, she didn't object. I just prayed this crazy ass girl didn't tear my house up.

I walked down the hall with Dreu following close behind. I told her where she'd be sleeping for the night. I also told her how to turn on the heater if she got cold. Living in Cali, we had the craziest weather. Our shit didn't get extremely hot like most states, in fact, it was always cold. I lived on the beach, so that only added to the cold breeze. During the summertime, it felt good at night, but that was only a couple months out the year.

"I just don't understand why y'all couldn't just drop me off," Dreu said, walking into the room.

"Because yo girl trying to get some dick tonight that's why."

"But, what that gotta do with me?"

"Man, just take yo stupid ass to sleep," I told her, then turned to walk away.

"Asshole," she said, but I didn't bother to turn around.

I went to the kitchen and looked for something easy to cook. Thanks to that crazy ass girl, we never even got a chance to order at the restaurant and a nigga was still starving.

East and his little boo thang had gone into the second guest room, so it was just me. I pulled out a New York steak that was already thawed out from this am. The pack contained two, so I decided to be nice and fix the other for Dreu. I threw the food into the skillet followed by mushrooms and onions. I dapped a little A1 sauce into the skillet then covered the meat. The sound of my phone alerted me I had a text, so I picked it up from the counter.

(323) 777-9311: *So, you just leave us all the way out here?*

Jazzy: *Hey sexy you ready for some company?*

Based on the first message, I knew it was Thing 1, so I ignored it.

Me: *wya?*
   Jazzy: *not far from you. I'm by the West Fields*
   Me: *aight pull up*

I told her then sat my phone back down. I knew I was gambling with my life because Dreu was right up the hall, but since she wanted to play hard, I was gonna show her ass. Out of all my bitches, Jazzy was the one I fucked with the most. She wanted a relationship, but I shot her down every chance I got. She was sexy as a muthafucka' and with some good pussy, but that wasn't the case. I had gone and done two with half in the county and Jazz was the first chick to come see me and was at every court date. She basically fought her way in because the first few months of my time, she was fighting left and right. When she realized her fighting wasn't gonna change shit, she stopped caring about all the other bitches.

To my surprise, she stayed down. But that still ain't change shit. Granted, I wouldn't be her nigga, but I did look out for her. I threw her a little bread when she needed, and I even took her on dates. But that was it.

As soon as Jazz knocked on the door, my mind drifted off to Dreu in the room. A nigga kinda felt bad for having Jazz over, but I needed some pussy. Just the thought of Dreu alone made my dick hard so I was gonna take it out on Jazz's pussy. I took her straight to my room, so I wouldn't risk them seeing each other. Normally, she would stay the night but tonight, I was gonna bust my nut and kick her right out.

FIVE

Dreu

I woke up out my sleep because I was having the craziest dream. I dreamed that Calhoun and I were outside on the beach making love by the ocean. The shit felt so real I actually bust a nut in my sleep. I lifted from the bed and went into the restroom that was connected to the bedroom I was sleeping in. I pulled off my panties and began to wash them out. Once I was done, I pulled a towel from the rack and began washing myself up.

After washing off the juices I caused myself, I went back to the bed to lay down. I wanted so bad to go find Calhoun, but I chose not to. Now that I had sobered up, I began thinking about everything that had transpired tonight and was slightly embarrassed. It was something about the way this nigga handled me that made my body crave him. I knew it sounded crazy, but when we fought outside the car, that shit turned me on more.

Just the thought of him made me spread my legs and touch myself. I closed my eyes and imagined it was him slowly rubbing my clit. I did this for some time until I made myself bust a nut. I tried my hardest to go to sleep, but I knew I would dream about this man again.

When I opened my eyes, it was now morning. I lifted from the bed and walked over to the window and looked out into the ocean. The view was so beautiful; I was quickly lost in my thoughts. I dreamed about life like this every day. I envisioned me as Calhoun's girl and living here enjoying the beach. I couldn't swim, but the whole scenery was life. Just the thought alone made me wanna grind harder. I wasn't no big time, but I was managing. I had to find out a way to put myself in a position like this. I wanted so bad to ask Calhoun what he did because I was sure he was a Dope Boy, but I didn't want to assume. I wouldn't mind a new connect, but I knew he wasn't gonna fuck with me because I was giving him a hard time.

"Come eat." I turned around to the sound of Calhoun's voice.

I didn't reply to him, but I did nod my head. I went into the restroom and searched under his cabinets for a toothbrush. Just like I thought, there was an entire pack with new brushes. I began brushing my teeth then washed my face. I took my time because I was a little nervous to go out there.

I walked out the room and headed into the kitchen in hopes to find Kaloni, so we could leave. I needed to get home because I had money to make. Just being here, told me I had to step my game up and that's exactly what I was gonna do.

"What's up, we leaving?" I looked at Kaloni.

"Good morning to you, too," she said, looking up from her food. I took a seat in front of what I assumed was my plate and picked up the piece of bacon that laid neatly.

"The way you were getting yo back blew out, I thought you would wake up on a better note," East said, smirking at me. I had no idea what he was talking about, but the look Calhoun shot him let me know exactly what.

"Wrong bitch," I shot, sarcastically.

A rage of jealousy came running through my body. I wanted so bad to jump across this table and punch his ass in the face. He tried so hard to avoid my eye contact, but I continued to grill his ass. I couldn't believe this nigga had fucked somebody while I was in this house. I know it sounded crazy because I wasn't his girl, but fuck that, we had a chemistry that was beyond crazy. Or so I thought.

"When we leaving?" I asked Kaloni but still grilling Calhoun.

"Y'all not," East said making me damn near break my neck.

"Fuck you mean we not?"

"Like he said shorty, we bout to roll out and y'all staying here for the day," Calhoun said. I was still salty with him, so I ignored him.

"She staying." I nodded my head to Kaloni and stood to my feet. "I'm out this bitch. I don't got no dick here and I got shit to do."

"Man, sit the fuck down Dreu before I get the fuck up. You hard headed as a muthafucka," Calhoun said with an evil glare.

"Just because I ain't submissive like her, nigga, don't mean I'm hardheaded."

I looked over at Kaloni. The look she wore told me I hurt her feelings. I didn't mean to, but it was true. She was being too submissive to a nigga she just met. I mean East was probably good for her and I could tell he liked her, but fuck that, they just met. I didn't want her to get hurt in the end because she didn't know this nigga background. I was the one that would have to console her, so she needed to listen to me.

"So, you're just gonna leave me?" she asked, looking sad. I wanted to say *yes bitch bye*, but I had already shitted on her once.

"I'm leaving first thing in the morning," I told her, then went into Calhoun's bedroom.

Moments later, the nigga came in questioning why was I in his room. I ignored his ass and continued looking through his drawers. He stood by the door watching me without a word and when I went into the third drawer, he ran up on me.

"The fuck you doing yo?"

"Looking for something to wear. Nigga, I hope you didn't think I was gonna sit in this house all fucking day in the same shit from last night." I crossed my hands over one another. "If you want I can just leave." I said as I rolled my eyes.

I was still salty about the chick he fucked, so when he got close to me, I moved so he wouldn't touch me. He rambled through his drawer and pulled out a pair of boxers and a white tee. He also threw me a pair of crisp white socks. I snatched the items from him and stormed to the guestroom. I was gonna shower and go give Kaloni a piece of my mind. But I was gonna wait until these niggas were gone.

～

"You're in love with him, Dreu, just stop being so rude to him."

"I'm not in love with him." I smacked my lips. "And he's the one that's rude."

"So, why you beat that girl ass?" she smirked, making me laugh.

"Cause the bitch was being disrespectful. I'm not trying to fuck with him. That nigga got bitches and I won't be added to his roster. But what's up with you and East? I see you digging on him."

"I like him. He's so nice to me."

"Yeah, just don't get caught up with that nigga Loni. Y'all moving a little fast."

"He makes me happy," she said with a pout. I looked out into the water, so I could find the right things to say without hurting her. I had to be careful when it came to her sensitive ass.

"Y'all moving kinda fast is all I'm saying. I'm not about to chastise you about it. I just want you to be careful with your heart. Loving a dope boy ain't easy." I told her seriously. "Where them niggas at anyway?" I asked, looking down at my phone. They had left this am and it was now nearly 7 pm.

"Let me find out you checking for your boo?" she smiled. "They went to handle some business."

"Oh," was all I said.

I focused my attention back on the currents of the ocean. For the last two hours, Loni and I sat outside on the beach just talking. I was trying hard to ease my mind, but I couldn't because all I thought about was Calhoun. This boy had me at hello. I'd never had these feelings over a guy. He was so damn sexy and cocky. Just the thought of him made my insides cringe. I couldn't wait until we left because I needed to get away from him and fast.

I focused my attention back to Loni and before I knew it, I was being scooped up off my feet. "Put me down!" I was kicking and screaming as Calhoun ran across the beach with me in his arms.

"Calhoun! No pleeeease!" I was yelling to the top of my lungs.

As we neared the water, my heart was pounding. He took me out into the water still holding me and I was ready to beat his ass. He wouldn't stop, so I was holding on to his neck for dear life. I could feel the water rising on my body, but I was too scared to look down.

"Calhoun, please." I begged, silently into his ear.

I still hadn't looked down, but I felt the water now covering my legs.

The moment I opened my eyes a big wave was coming for us. Suddenly it crashed into us knocking us under water. The currents began to take me, and I knew my life was over. I tried to open my eyes under water, but I couldn't see a thing. I tried my best to swim, but I failed.

"Dreu!" I heard Calhoun calling my name, but I couldn't see him.

Finally, I reached out and I could feel his body near mine, so I grabbed him. He scooped me up into his arms and I instantly began to choke. I had water up my nose and mouth. As soon as I got over this shit, I was gonna sock his stupid ass for playing so much.

Calhoun walked me into the house and the minute we touched the wooden flooring I jumped down and stormed into the guest bedroom. I was so upset, I wanted to just get my shit and go. I didn't give a fuck if I had to walk, I was getting the fuck away from this dumb ass nigga.

"What you so butt hurt for?" Calhoun said, walking into the room.

I played it off like I was gonna walk out then reached over and punched his ass. When I connected, I started swinging wildly, making sure I hit his ass a few more times before he knocked me out. Fed up with my assault, Calhoun slapped me, sending me flying into the dirty clothes hamper. I grabbed my face and ran up on him again. This time he caught me and shoved me down to the ground. I tried to jump up and tackle his ass, but I was too slow. I flew head first into the dresser then laid out. The room was so silent the only thing could be heard was the sound of me and Calhoun's breathing. When he walked over to me, he picked me up from the ground and laid me on the bed. I was still soaking wet, but he didn't seem to mind. Next thing I know, he pulled down the wet briefs I was wearing then moved to my shirt.

"I can't swim," I said as tears began to fall from my eyes.

"I didn't know baby," Calhoun said and kissed my lips. I was so out of it, I didn't realize what was going on until I noticed he wasn't wearing any clothes.

He began tracing kisses down my neck causing a waterfall in between my legs. I flinched when he reached my face because of the scar I now had from him. When I say he slapped the taste out my mouth, I meant it. I guess he noticed what he had done because he kissed it softly.

"Stop fighting me ma," he said, breathing hard into my ear.

Just the sound of his voice made my body do things I never thought they would do. My legs opened wider, inviting him inside of me. He looked me in the eyes and I guess it was the confirmation he needed, because he grabbed his dick and put the tip at my opening.

For a few moments, Calhoun tried easing his way in. I hadn't noticed how big he was until now. Finally making his way inside of me, I could feel him invading my love box slowly. My walls clasped around his dick, making him moan out my name.

"Ohhh." I let out a sexy moan that I assumed drove him crazy because he looked at me with so much fire in his eyes. It was crazy how my body seemed so familiar with him. It's like my pussy was made for him and him only.

"I'mma make you mine, watch," he said as he stroked slowly.

I wish what he said was true at this moment, but it wasn't. This nigga was gassing me because my pussy was good to him. I wasn't no fool.

Tired of making love to a nigga I wasn't in love with, I began to fuck him from the bottom. When he tried to kiss me again, I moved my face because I had snapped back to myself.

"Ohhhh shit," I cried out.

This nigga dick was like heaven sent. Just the thought of me being hooked, made me wanna stop. My eyes began to get watery again because I hated how he was making me feel.

"Stop tripping baby girl, I'm here," he said, sensing my mood change. *For how long nigga?* I thought in my feelings again. I was up and down with him and it only confused me more.

Calhoun and I went at it for some time before the nigga finally bust his nut. I had already nutted four times, but I still wanted to go at it. He rolled off of me and laid beside me breathing hard. I stood to my feet and went into the restroom. I slammed the door and began to cry my eyes out. One would think I was bipolar, but I was suffering from lack of love. I wanted so bad to be loved, but I was scared. Other than Loni, my little brother, and my grandma I had nobody in my life that loved me, so I was scared to let anyone in. I wasn't no fool to street niggas, I knew Calhoun would only hurt me so after today, I was gonna leave and crawl back into my shell.

SIX

East

———

"You're always gone baby. I miss you." Jennifer whined wrapping her arms around me.

"I know baby, but a nigga been working," I said as I kissed her on the forehead.

For the last week, I had been handling my business in the traps and spending time with Kaloni, so I was beginning to neglect my girl. I felt bad as fuck just looking at her, but I couldn't help it. Kaloni was doing something to me that Jennifer had done when we first met. Being with her was like the breath of air I needed. She wasn't the typical hood chick that complained when I didn't call, which made me blow her shit up.

For some reason, I always wanted to be around her, and that shit was interfering with my relationship. I don't know where Kaloni and I were going with this, but I had to figure shit out. Both women were innocent in this and I didn't want to hurt either. I was caught the fuck up for the first time in my life because all the other chicks I cheated with never had this effect on me. I didn't want to risk losing Jennifer who I had been with for years for a chick that I had just met. But on the other hand, I didn't want to miss out on Kaloni's loving. Kaloni and I laid up and talked about everything under the sun. Not saying Jennifer didn't have great conversation, but what was there to really talk about. Most of the time, she was always into her phone, gone, or buried into her computer.

"When you coming back?" she asked with a pout.

I couldn't do shit but laugh. She was my baby and I'd die if I lost her. Just looking at her pretty face made me wanna just stay home, but I had shit to do.

Jennifer was bad hands down. She had a pretty light complexion and light grey eyes she inherited from her mother. She had a banging ass body that looked almost fake. That was the difference between her and Kaloni. Kaloni was nice and petite with a little round booty that fit in the palm of my hand perfectly. She didn't have the breast Jenn had, but in my eyes, they were perfect. Another thing about Jenn was she didn't work, which was why she complained about me being home. She had too much time on her hands. Upon talking to Kaloni, she told me about her job at Walgreens. Although the job was shitty, I still gave it to baby girl for trying.

"I'll be back in a couple hours ma. I gotta handle some shit with Cali."

"Umm," she said out of annoyance because she couldn't stand Cali.

She knew Cali had bitches and he wasn't ready to settle down, but what she didn't understand was, I was my own man. I didn't do the shit Cali did because I had my own mind. Let Jen tell it, we were flipping bitches together and kept different woman running in and out our traps.

"Don't start," I told her, standing to my feet.

I kissed her again and made my way for the door. When I turned around, she stood there looking sad.

"I love you," I told her to assure her. When the huge smile crept up on her face, it made it easier for me to leave.

"I love you more," she said just as the door was closing. I hopped into my car and made my way to Wing Stop. I was gonna take Kaloni some lunch before meeting up with Cali.

After getting the food, I headed in the direction of Kaloni's job. When I pulled up, I headed in and spotted her behind the register. She was smiling hard, greeting a customer; she never noticed me. I stood back admiring her pretty ass smile. When she finally looked up, she looked surprised to see me. It'd been a couple days since we chilled because I had to go spend time with Jenny.

I held the bag of food up to let her know I had brought her lunch. She gave me the one finger to let me know give her a minute, so I walked back out to my whip to make some calls.

Fifteen minutes later, Kaloni came out and climbed into my whip. She reached over and placed a kiss on my cheek. I could tell she was excited to see me, and the feelings were mutual. I handed her the bag of food and informed her the root beer was hers. I didn't have to tell her twice because she tore into the bag without saying a word.

"Thank you, babe. I was starving," she said, shoving a French fry into her mouth. "So, where you been stranger?" she asked, as she lifted the paper to get to her lemon pepper wings.

"Girl it's only been two days," we both laughed. "But a nigga been working," I lied.

I never told Kaloni about Jennifer for numerous of reasons. I would eventually tell her, but I wasn't worried about her finding out. Kaloni didn't seem like the snooping type and Jenny was a home-body, so I didn't have to worry about them running into each other. I had Jenn staked out in Ladera Heights while Kaloni lived in the hood in the heart of South Central. When the time came to make things official, I was gonna move her across town. First, I had to see where her head was at.

"Damn baby yo ass was starving," I said, playfully and laughed.

"I was," she said and dropped her head.

"Why haven't you eaten?"

"I don't know, East. I really don't have money like that to eat out every day," she responded and dropped her head again.

I could tell she was embarrassed, and it made me feel bad. I went into my pocket and pulled out five crisp one hundreds. I tried to hand her the money, but she wouldn't take it.

"I can't take that. I'm fine."

"Man, you not fine. Fuck I look like letting my girl starve." At just the mention of her being my girl, made her eyes light up.

"I'm yo girl now?" she asked with a smirk.

"Yeah, shit. You didn't know," I said and pushed the money into her uniform top. "That should hold you over for lunch the rest of the week."

"Thank youuuu."

"Your welcome, now get back in there and get to work."

"Okay, but will I see you tonight?" she asked unsure.

I wanted to tell her no because I really needed to go home, but I didn't want to disappoint her so I nodded my head yes. She smiled, then hopped out the car. I started my car up and pulled out the lot. Before I made it fully out the lot, I had a text come through my phone.

Kaloni: *thank you again. (smiley face)*
   Me: *no need to thank me but you welcome ma*

I strolled into the warehouse feeling good. I don't know why, but it was something about Loin's presence that put my mind to ease. I couldn't wait for her to get off work because I really needed to holler at her. I wanted to talk about her personal life, so I could get a better understanding. Hearing her tell me today she couldn't afford to buy herself lunch made me wanna give her the world. I could tell by her appearance she wasn't one of those material girls, but being on my arm shit was gonna change. Don't get me wrong, she dressed nice and took great care of herself, but she was too simple. She always wore jeans and simple shoes like chucks and vans.

Since I had pretty much made shit official with her, I was oblig-ated to do things for her. I wasn't no trick or nothing, but if I claimed you as mine, you had to shine like a diamond because I was. I wasn't no flashy type nigga, but everybody knew me and knew I was paid. I dressed fresh as fuck, so I couldn't have no chick representing me that wasn't out here shitting too. Things for Kaloni was about to change I just hoped her ass was prepared.

"Sup, E" I slapped hands with the homie Benji.

Benji was one of my workers, but more of a homie. He chose his position in the damn warehouse over the traps so that's what he got. He had been working for us for some years and to be real, he was the most trusted nigga from the camp.

"Benji, what's shaking?"

"Shit yo boy in there and he on one," Benji said, nodding towards the door. "I'm bout to step out and smoke a cigarette. He stressing me out shit," he said, walking out and closing the door behind him.

When I stepped into the warehouse, Cali was pacing the floor and talking shit to the ladies that was bagging up our work. Our warehouse is where everything got done. We had a room where everything got cooked by either Me or Cali. We had another room where shit got weighed, which Benji was in charge of. We also had a room where the ladies packaged our shit naked. I know y'all thinking these niggas watch too much damn New Jack City and y'all damn right. If these bitches didn't wear no clothes, they couldn't steal. After taking so many loses, we had to tighten up.

"I got fifteen birds cooked up, so why the fuck is there only one packaged? The shit been cooked since Tuesday and today is fucking Friday. Now, I don't have a problem with hiring new staff in this bitch, so if y'all don't tighten the fuck up, I'mma fire all y'all asses!"

"Who pissed in this nigga cereal?" Lonyell reached over and whispered in my ear.

Lonyell had been working for us for a little over a year and ever since Cali started fucking her, she got away with certain things. But the way he was looking today, I could tell he wasn't playing with her, so I stepped away from her.

"Lonyell, since you wanna play games like I'm a fucking joke, bring yo stupid ass here." Cali got dead in on her ass.

She walked over to where he stood, ass swanging and tities dangling. I couldn't help but to look. She had one of those natural asses that you could sit a 5th of Hennessy bottle on. Her face was decent, but nothing to stare at too hard. Now that ass was to die for.

"Drop down and suck my dick," Cali told her making everyone in the room gasp.

"What?" she asked him just as shocked as I was.

See that was Lonyell's problem, she was too damn privileged. I knew he was doing this to show her she wasn't shit like the rest of them. What I didn't understand was, why the fuck did she think she was different? This nigga fucked her in this warehouse and hadn't even taken her on a simple date.

"Bitch if you don't drop down now, you can kiss yo job good-bye," he told her without blinking.

She slowly got on her knees hoping he'll change his mind, but that nigga wasn't playing with her.

"You know who I do shit like this too?" he asked her, and she shook her head no. "Hoes! This how I treat hoes. Now any bitch in here think she better than the next, gone get dogged the fuck out. I don't know why this simple ass bitch thought she was special enough to play games with me," he said shoving his dick back in his pants while looking at the other girls. "Get the fuck back to work," he told her shoving her out his face. "When I come back in this muthafucka I better see some fucking progress, or everybody fucking fired." He stormed out the room and into what we referred to as the kitchen.

The kitchen consisted of two stoves, a table, and restaurant fridge that held only water and about a hundred boxes of baking soda.

When I walked in, Cali was already coming out his shirt ready to get to work. At times, he would cook at home so him being here today meant we were gonna be working for hours.

"Man, what's up with you?" I asked, walking over to the fridge to grab some baking soda then over to my stove.

"Shit, just a lot going on. These simple bitches got a simple job and can't even do the shit right." He slammed the pot on top of the stove. "Then this weird ass bitch Dreu playing with a nigga," he said making me look over at him.

This what's wrong with his ass; I thought staring dead at the nigga.

"So, this what's wrong with yo ass?"

"Man fuck her," he tried to brush me off.

"Nah nigga. You open for that bitch."

"Don't call her that nigga. I don't disrespect yo bucket head ass little boo," he said making me laugh.

"I don't understand what's the problem. Y'all both feeling each other."

"That's the problem. I hit her with this dope dick and the bitch gone tell me she not ready to be in a relationship." He shook his head. "Can you believe this shit?"

"So, you basically got friendzoned?" I had to stop cooking because I was laughing so hard.

"Fuck you nigga."

"My bad bro. So, what you gonna do?"

"Shit. the bitch wanna play games I got something for her ass."

"Well, nigga maybe she think you gone break her heart. Have you asked her her story? Like what's she's been through with men."

"No. Fuck I'mma ask her that for?" he frowned his face.

"Nigga, you gotta ask these types of things. It will show you interested in her. This the type of shit girls like. I'mma tell you my nigga, that girl looked broken like she been through some thangs."

"Nigga, you know I don't know about this relationship shit," he said and wasn't lying. The closest he got to a relationship was with this chick names Ayanna. He had a fake relationship with Jazzy, but she got dissed on a regular.

"Well, if you plan on fucking with her, you better tighten up," I told him, and the sound of his phone ringing made him look down.

"Mari ass," he said looking back up.

"How lil sis doing?"

"She good. I'mma take her out to eat tonight. You wanna roll?"

"I'm supposed to hook up with Kaloni, but shit, we'll roll with y'all."

"Yeah, see if my baby wanna come," he said smirking.

Cali and I chopped it up for the next few hours. We were supposed to cook up five bricks, but Mari's spoiled ass kept calling saying she was hungry. We wrapped it up and departed. I went to scoop Kaloni and Dreu up and he went to get Mari. We agreed to hit up this restaurant called *Kan I Get A Plate*. The food was good as fuck and the restaurant made you feel at home. The cook *Chef Neecee* was cool too. She played Trap music when you dined inside and had a Xbox hook up in a lounge area.

SEVEN

Calhoun

_____

*P*ulling up to the restaurant, I found a parking spot in the front then looked over at Mari who was putting on her makeup. I couldn't understand for the life of me why she was wearing the shit because she had a natural beauty. She didn't cake it on, but still she didn't need that shit.

"Hurry up man."

"Bye. I don't need you to wait for me."

"Man, just hurry up," I told her and got out the car. I stood to the side and waited for Mari to finish, which took her another ten minutes.

Noticing East whip, I sped up my pace because I was anxious to see Dreu. I hadn't seen her since the night we fucked because she was dodging a nigga. East had told me where she lived because he had picked Kaloni up there before. Every time I pulled by, an older lady told me she wasn't there. I knew she was getting my messages, but her ass was stubborn. She didn't work so I didn't understand what was she always doing in the streets.

"Sup y'all? Sup Dreu." I said, and she rolled her eyes. I laughed it off and took a seat.

"Sup sis?" East greeted Mari as she also took her seat.

When I sat down, I picked up the menu and everyone did the same except Dreu. She was sitting there with her arms folded across her chest mugging me. I don't know what the fuck was this girl's problem, but she seriously had one.

"What you getting babygirl?" I asked Mari.

"You know what I'm getting," she laughed. This was her favorite spot and she always got the mango chicken, with rice and string beans.

"That's all you get," I told her, shaking my head. The sound of Dreu smacking her lips made me look up from my menu. I guess she wanted some attention.

"What you eating ma?"

She smacked her lips again before replying.

"Don't worry bout me, worry bout yo little bitch," she said, mugging Mari.

"Who she talking to?" Mari looked at me then back to Dreu.

"I'm talking to..."

"Dreu, chill ma." I told her, before she went crazy.

She jumped up from the table like a spoiled bitch. When I noticed Kaloni about to get up to get her, I told her don't trip I had her.

I went outside and Dreu was standing in the front on her phone. By the way she was looking, I could tell she calling a ride. I assumed it had to be Uber because I was sure she wasn't dumb enough to call no nigga to come get her. Right when I was about to step to her, her phone rang. The smile that crept up on her face had me hot. She was so busy smiling, and acting like I wasn't even right here, but she had me fucked up.

"Where you at?" the nigga on the phone asked her.

"I'm at Kan I get a..." before she could finish, I snatched the phone out her hand.

"Give me my phone, Cali!" She was trying to fight me.

"Man watch out," I told her ready to knock fire from her ass.

"She busy my nigga. She gotta talk to you some other time," I told the nigga and hung up on his ass. She snatched her phone from me and it began ringing again..

"On my dead mama, you answer that phone I'm beat yo ass."

"Nigga you got yo fucking nerves. Yo bitch sitting up in there." She looked mad as fuck.

"Man, you dumb as fuck."

"How the fuck I'm dumb? This the third fucking time," she shouted and looked like she wanted to cry.

"Man, what the fuck you talking about?"

"Nigga, you know what I'm talking about. First, the bitch in the club who ass I had to beat at the Deli, then you fuck a bitch while I'm at the fucking house." As soon as the words left her mouth, I felt like shit. She walked up on me and her crazy ass tried to swing on me. I grabbed her hands to block her shot.

"That's my fucking sister in there!" I told her, because she was about to go into a rage. When I confessed Mari was my sibling, she stopped swinging then dropped her head.

"Man, yo ass gone go in there an apologize to her. I'll get my apology later when I pick yo ass up." I told her then slapped her on the ass.

To my surprise, she didn't hesitate. She walked her ass right into the restaurant and back to our table.

"It's okay," Mari smiled.

I was really shocked because if y'all thought Dreu was an asshole, y'all had not seen Mari in action. That girl hated every bitch I brought around except Jazzy. And the only reason she liked Jazzy, was because Jazzy gave her any and everything even when I said no. I was glad they had let this shit go because Dreu was gonna be around for a while. Once I got her ass to act right, I was gonna follow East instructions and get to know her. Just looking at her right now, I couldn't believe I was about to say this, but baby girl was the one. It was crazy as fuck how her exterior was so innocent, but her interior was like a raging fucking bull. I was gonna break her down and that was my mission.

~

Walking out the restaurant, Dreu was a little more relaxed. Her, Kaloni and Mari were indulged in a girly conversation, while East and I lingered in the background chopping it up about our work. The girls had walked over by my whip, so I followed East to his ride. We needed to figure some shit out about this new spot we were about to open and that nigga Dee who had still been stepping on our toes. For days, I watched that nigga spot and not a trace of him. My next mission was to just burn the crib down.

"So, what you gonna do?" East asked, as if he was reading my mind.

"I'mma burn the nigga spot down," I replied, nonchalantly. He started laughing at me and I didn't see shit funny. I was dead ass serious.

"Cali!" I turned around to the sound a chick calling me.

When I looked up, it was this chick named Frenisha. She walked over to me looking good as a muthafucka. I was so into how fat Frenisha ass looked in her Burberry jeans, I forgot all about Dreu.

Dreu came walking towards us with a scowl on her face. I knew how this shit was about to go, so I looked at Frenisha unsure about what I was gonna say.

Fuck it, I thought as I grabbed Dreu's hand and pulled her close to me.

"Frenisha, this my girl. Baby this the homegirl," I introduced the two.

"Homegirl?" Frenisha dumbass said making me eye her stupid ass. She didn't want them problems with Dreu, so I needed her to shut the fuck up. "Cali got a girlfriend? They must have issued ice water in hell," Frenisha said, laughing at her own dumb ass joke.

"Exactly what I...."

Pop! Pop! Pop! Pop! Pop! Pop! Pop! Pop! Pop! Pop! Pop! Pop! Pop! Pop! Pop!

The sound of gunfire filled the air, making me dive for Dreu. When I knew she was good, I wiped out my strap and began to fire back.

Rat! tat! tat! Rat! tat! Tat! Rat! tat! Tat! Rat! tat! Tat! Rat! tat! Tat! Rat! tat! Tat! Rat! tat! Tat! Rat! tat! Tat!

I ran towards the car as I emptied my entire clip. When I was done shooting, I ran to make sure Mari and Kaloni were straight. They were both using my car as a shield and Kaloni was crying her eyes out.

This chick too damn soft yo; I shook my head.

I ran back over to Dreu and she was bleeding from the knee. East was good, but Frenisha wasn't. She laid in a pool of her own blood facedown. *Damn;* I thought looking at her lifeless body.

"Oh, my God nooo." Kaloni walked over screaming.

"Get in the car!" I told Kaloni, as I snatched Dreu up.

"We can't just leave her."

"Man, get yo ass in the car!" I could hear East and Kaloni going back and forth.

When I made it to my car, Dreu had ran to the driver's seat and Mari jumped into the back. I got in the passenger's seat and instructed Dreu to drive out to my crib in the West, so we could drop Mari off. Her ass sped off like we were running from the police, but it didn't faze me because I drove like a bat out of hell.

Pulling up to my crib, we let Mari out and I told her I'd be back to take her shopping in a couple days. She kissed me on the cheek and told Dreu she would call her. That shit really blew me back because clearly, they had exchanged numbers. The sound of Dreu's phone alerted her, so she reached into her hand bag and pulled it out. It was a text message and the way she read it puzzled me because she had frowned up. It wasn't my business, so I brushed it off and told her to drive out to the warehouse.

The ride to the warehouse was silent because I was contemplating my next move. First, I had to find out who the fuck it was, which wouldn't be hard because the streets talked. Once I did find out, shit was about to get ugly. Whoever the fuck it was, was about to feel my rapture. My little sister was with me, so the shit had me hot. I did my best to keep Mari away from shit like this because I had seen to many innocent people killed. I don't know who the fuck was gunning for me, because the streets feared me. Whoever had beef with me was too scared to make a move so this shit was puzzling.

"We bout to run in here real quick, then I'mma drop you off," I told Dreu as we pulled up to the warehouse.

"You not dropping me off," she quickly replied.

"Man, it's not up for discussion. You saw what happened today and I don't want shit to happen to you. Look at yo fucking pants," I told her, referring to the blood that had seeped through her jeans.

"It's nothing but a scrape." She shrugged her shoulders. "I'm still not leaving you, so I guess we bout to roll out together."

I looked at her to see was she for real and she was. I couldn't do shit but shake my head. This girl was a tough cookie bro I swear. The shit turned me the fuck on.

EIGHT

Kaloni

---

*E*ast and I pulled up to an unknown location that we followed Dreu and Cali, too. I was still shaken up, so I wanted to go home, but I didn't want to look like a wimp. I still had tears in my eyes from what went on at the restaurant. Just seeing that poor girl laid out on the ground covered in blood still played in my head. I couldn't believe they left her like that. I prayed over a thousand times she'd be okay, but deep down inside, I knew she wouldn't. I had never in my life witnessed anything like this. Dreu was cut for this shit, but I wasn't. Now I understood why she was so overprotective of me and especially, why she didn't want me to be with East. *His damn lifestyle.*

"Look ma, I hate you had to be there for that shit and ain't nothing I could say to make you feel better. But to keep shit one hunnit with you, we don't be beefing with niggas. This city belongs to me and Cali. Everybody fears us"

"I'm not from the *hood* East," I told him as tears came down my face again. "I understand you're probably used to *Ride or Die* females, but I'm not one. Just because I live in the hood, don't mean

I'm hood. My life consists of going to work, chilling in my room with my best friend, and helping her little brother with homework," I cried harder.

I hated to be so weak, but this shit just wasn't me.

"Fucking with a nigga like me ain't easy. I sell dope for a fucking living, Kaloni!" he shouted, nearly scaring me.

I couldn't do shit but stare at him because all this time, I didn't know what he'd done for a living. Dreu mentioned he had to be a hustla and she was right.

"Shit like this gonna happen. Now, I understand if you don't wanna fuck with me, but if you do, I promise I'll do everything I can to keep you out of harm's way," he told me so sincerely, but I didn't know if I was ready to be a *Dope Boys* wife. My life was simple. Hell, Dreu called me Granny for Christ sakes.

"Let's go up in here and I'mma take you home soon as I'm done," he said not giving me a chance to object.

I really wanted to sit in the car because honestly the place looked creepy as hell. *I guess I don't have a choice;* I thought climbing out of the car. The only thing that made me feel secure was when I saw Dreu get out the car with Cali, so I felt more at ease.

When we walked into what East and Cali had referred to as the warehouse, I was shitting bricks. There were two guys at the door holding huge guns. I snuggled underneath East as he guided us through. He walked us to a room that had a couch and a table and told Drue and I to hold tight. East and Cali had made their way into the huge warehouse and Dreu and I began chattering about today's event.

"This exactly why I told yo ass not to fuck with him." She looked at me shaking her head. I really didn't know what to say because she was right. "Look, Kaloni, if you gone fuck with him, I suggest you get it together. You think this is all you're gonna experience? Well, guess what? It's not. Trust me baby girl, you ain't ready for this shit." She shot not making the situation any better.

"But, I really like him," I said on a verge of crying again.

It was true. I really liked East. After what he had done today, really made me fall for him. The money he had given me was just a bonus. I was more infatuated with the fact he took time out his day to bring me lunch. Every time he called me, he would ask was I okay. He would send me text when we weren't together just to say he missed me, or he was thinking about me. Despite East being street, he was charming. We talked about so many things that I would never expect him to talk about. I knew he was a busy man because his phone constantly rang. However, when he was in my presence, he would ignore the call and give me his undivided attention.

"Well, you better get ready for the ride," she said, then looked down at her phone.

"Who's that?" I asked because her face frowned up.

"Brick," she replied, then going back to text. I shook my head at her because she was crazy as hell.

"Cali, gone hurt you."

"Fuck, Cali."

"You're crazy. He really likes you, Dreu. I saw when he dove to save you today. Why do you give him such a hard time?" She looked at me and contemplated her words.

"You know how I am, Loni. I don't let my guards down. And anyway, if I give in too easy, he'll think he got me. I can't have that," she said smiling.

"So, what's up with this Brick nigga?"

"Brick, is just Brick. I mean he cool, but he got too much going on for me."

"Oh," was all I said, because like I always say, if she wanted me to know she would tell me. She had mentioned Brick to me a few times, but from what she said was, it wasn't nothing major. She had been dealing with him for some time now, but just like Cali, she wouldn't give him a chance.

"I gotta pee," I told her, shaking my leg.

"Let's go find the guys," she replied and lifted from the sofa.

We walked out the door running right into a guy that was so huge we had to look up at him.

"Didn't East tell y'all sit the fuck down?"

"East ain't my fucking daddy, he hers. And since yo' ass so fucking nosey, we gotta piss," Dreu said and kept walking.

"You can't go..." the guy shouted, but Dreu ignored him.

I followed behind her as she walked into the double doors. When we reached inside, my eyes grew wide at what I saw in front of me. The guy ran in and Cali motioned for him to chill. You could tell he was mad, but he didn't go against Cali's orders. Walking fully into the room, I began to look around. The room looked like a laboratory. There were about ten long tables filled with drugs. Standing in front of the tables were naked women in white mask and gloves. Everyone in the room looked over towards us including East and Cali. I looked at Dreu and she didn't seem moved by what was taking place. I wanted so bad to run out, but East motioned for me to come to him.

"So, this what y'all be up to. Let a bitch get a job baby," Dreu said to Cali as she walked around the warehouse. When she walked past one table, I noticed a girl mugging her. I assumed Dreu noticed it too because she turned around to grill the chick.

"Fuck you looking at bitch, get to work," Dreu told the girl making me and East chuckle.

"Dreu, get yo ass over here," Cali told her.

Dreu smirked walking back past the chick and made her way towards us. East whispered in my ear that we were gonna leave soon and I couldn't wait. I needed to get in my bed and call it a day. Shit was crazy today, and finding out the operation East and Cali ran, it got even crazier.

East

I took Kaloni home and instead of leaving, I went inside. I wanted to lay with her and make her forget about everything that happened today. I could tell she was shaken up and not to mention, seeing the operation Cali and I had at the warehouse really had her looking crazy. I really didn't want her to see no shit like that but her ass just couldn't sit still. Judging by her friend Dreu, one would think she was a little tougher, but nah. Baby girl was green, and I was gonna change that. Don't get me wrong, I didn't want her on no thug shit, but I wanted her to understand my lifestyle.

She needed to know if shit ever happened, she couldn't ball up crying. I needed her to know what to do. I guess this is why I was happy I had Jenn because she had adapted to my lifestyle fast. She wasn't as green as Kaloni, but she was ditsy. I broke her down and now the crazy girl carried a gun and even knew to post bail if need be.

Speaking of the devil; I thought as my phone rang. Jenn had called me three times and I let it go to voicemail. Kaloni shot me a look like *answer yo phone,* but I couldn't. I still hadn't told her about Jenn and especially now I refused, too. She already looked at me as some drive by, dope selling, street nigga, so I didn't want her to think I was a cheating sack of shit even though I was.

"Where yo mom?" I asked, Kaloni as we walked into her room.

"No telling," she said, sadly.

I looked around her room and I couldn't front, I was impressed. Her shit was decorated nicely, and I could tell she was clean. The rest of the house was cool, too, but it reeked of cigarettes.

"I'm bout to take a nap." I kicked my shoes off and laid down in her bed.

"Why you ain't answering yo phone?"

"It's Cali," I lied. "Come lay down.

I told her and pat the side of me. She smiled and came to lay down. As soon as she laid down, I started rubbing her leg. I told her take her clothes off and she did as told. Through her shirt, I could see her hard ass nipples and that's all I needed to see.

When she took her shirt off, her pretty ass perky titties stood at attention. I took one into my mouth and sucked on it like a newborn being breastfed.

"Ea..." she moaned so sexily the shit made my dick harder.

I stood up and pulled my pants down. I then took off my shirt because I was about to dive in dick first. She watched me from the bed and I could tell she was nervous. I climbed in bed with her and began fondling her again. When I stuck my hands between her legs, she was wet as fuck. I began to play with her clit making her moan loud as hell. I slid my finger into her pussy and it was nice and tight. Not being able to hold back, I lift her up and guided her to my dick. She did a squat on top of me, so I brought her down slowly.

"Ahhhhh." She frowned up and let out a moan at the same time.

"This pussy gone be mine forever baby?" I asked, but more so telling her. I wasn't gonna let Kaloni go rather she liked it or not.

"Yesss, baby…ohhh yes." She let out a cry like moan. That's all I needed to hear. I started pounding inside of her from the bottom as I held onto her waist for dear life.

"What the hell?" I heard a voice, so I looked around Kaloni's room.

I guess she was so in tune, she didn't hear shit. When she finally turned around, she grabbed the sheet and pulled it over us.

"Mom!"

"Don't mom me. Y'all nasty asses doing the freak nasty in my house."

"My bad moms," I told her, then lifted up to slide my clothes on.

"Yeah, yo bad nigga. I hope you got something for me," Kaloni mom said then left the room. I shook my head because I knew exactly what she meant; she wanted some work.

"Yo' moms something else," I told Kaloni sliding into my shoes.

"Oh, my god, I'm so embarrassed," she said and dropped her head.

"Ain't shit to be embarrassed about ma. Next time just lock the door." I chuckled to try and lighten the mood. "I gotta roll anyway. I'mma see you tomorrow baby girl okay?"

"Okay," she said with a head nod. I kissed her forehead then left the room.

When I got into the living room, her mom was sitting on the sofa. Her foot was shaking, and she wore a look that said *nigga run my shit*. I shook my head again and reached into my pocket. If Kaloni knew what I was about to do, she would kill me, but I felt bad she had caught us. I pulled out the sandwich bag with the work I carried just to pay smokers when they did shit for me, then handed her a nice fat dub rock. She took the drugs eagerly, and then ran off to the back of the house. I headed out the door, but I made a pact with myself that I wouldn't do it again. If Loni found out, she would be pissed and that's something I didn't need.

I jumped into my whip and dialed Jenn as I pulled off. On the second ring, she answered like she had been waiting for my call.

"Six hours later?" she asked, upon answering the phone.

"I was in the kitchen," I told her referring to the room in the warehouse where I cooked.

"Anything could have been wrong Elijah."

"Well, is it?" I asked, already getting annoyed.

"No but damn," she smacked her lips. "You know this the same shit you were doing when you were out fucking with bitches. Let me find out."

"Find out what? A nigga just hustling."

"I'm not dumb my nigga."

"You must be. What's up, though?"

"Nothing, damn, I was just checking in with you. I started to think…"

"You ain't think shit, but I was with a bitch. That's all you think about."

"But you gave me reasons to."

"Man, I ain't did shit in years. Leave the past in the past."

"And you leave the hoeing for Cali."

"Cali ain't got shit to do with this. You always bringing my nigga up and that shit starting to piss me off."

"He ain't shit and birds of a feather flock together," she shot, pissing me off.

"So, I guess hoes of a feather hoe together, then right? Because Regina a hoe and that's yo friend."

"My friend not a hoe."

"Three of my homies fucked including Cali, so that bitch is as good as a hoe."

"You know what, I'm not about to do this with you."

"And you know what. I'm not about to come home to you. Fuck off my phone." I hung up and bust a U Turn. I headed back to Kaloni's house where I could get a piece of mind. This was the exact reason I said Kaloni was a breath of fresh air.

"Grab a bag and let's roll, I'm in the front," I told Kaloni as soon as she answered.

We were gonna head to a room that I would check in for two days. I was gonna use this argument as my excuse, so I could wine and dine Loni and get her back into my good graces.

WANT A CHANCE TO WIN SOME CASH?

THE REAL DOPEBOYZ SERIES STARTED THIS WEEK. THERE WILL BE BOOKS FROM DIFFERENT AUTHORS THAT TAKE PLACE IN DIFFERENT PLACES AROUND THE WORLD.

SHAN PRESENTS CASH SCAVENGER HUNT.
1ST PLACE $400
2ND PLACE $275
3RD PLACE $150
4TH PLACE $100
5TH PLACE $75

IN EACH BOOK, THERE WILL BE 2 ITEMS TO COLLECT TO ADD TO YOUR TREASURE. AT THE END OF THE CONTEST, EMAIL ALL OF THE ITEMS THAT YOU FOUND TO SPREADINGCONTESTS@GMAIL.COM

IN THIS BOOK THE ITEMS ARE A CALIFORNIA SYMBOL AND A FAMOUS MOVIE WE SHOULD ALL KNOW.

NINE

Dreu

"So, are you going to the annual block party?" Mari asked me as we walked through the mall.

"Is your brother gonna be there? If not, I'll go."

"Of course, he is. He's the one who throws it. They also have giveaways for kids. You should bring your brother."

"I don't know. I'm really not trying to be around your brother like that."

"Girl you love him. Stop fronting," she said, making me turn beet red. I couldn't front, I was crushing hard on that man. Everything about him drove me crazy. Especially, after I seen him shoot that gun the other day. That shit was sexy as fuck.

"Okay, can I let you in on secret?"

"Sure."

"I really do like him. I'm just scared to be hurt. I don't have a torn past relationship or nothing, I just never been loved. I don't even know how to love a man," I said embarrassed.

"Well, that makes two of y'all. Anthony has never been in love. Nigga ain't never brought a girl home," she said, and we stopped walking. "Dreu, you gotta take chances in life. You'll never find love if you keep blocking people out of your life."

"You're right, it's just hard," I admitted.

Cali struck me as the type of nigga that had multiple women and children running around. I just know this nigga had been married multiple times.

"Just give him a chance, Dreu. He's really a sweet guy. And I'm not saying it because he's my brother," she said and we both giggled.

I enjoyed being around Mari. She had a great vibe and I could tell she was much mature than her age. I didn't have to be so tough around her unlike Kaloni. With Kaloni it was like I was the protector. I had to be tough to let her know, no one would fuck with her.

"Baby there's Mari." Mari and I both looked over at the same time. Some chick was smiling ear to ear as she made her way over towards us. *Baby?* I questioned as Cali stood there with a shocked look.

"Hey, Jazzy," Mari said, then looking over at me.

"Who's this, your friend?" she asked Mari. "Hey," she smiled, cheerfully. I rolled my eyes at her ass then focused in on Cali.

"What's up, Anthony?" I said to Cali, as I cracked my knuckles.

I couldn't wait until we got behind closed doors because I was gonna beat the fuck out of him. The nigga looked scared as hell. I nearly lost it when he hit me with a head nod.

"This exactly why I don't fuck with yo hoe ass," I mugged him. "Mari catch a ride with your brother, I'll see you later," I told her then walk away.

The moment my feet hit the pavement, I don't know why, but I began running. I needed to get far away from the mall because my heart couldn't stand to see Cali and that chick again. See this was the exact reason I couldn't fuck with this nigga. He constantly complained about a relationship, but yet and still, he always did fuck shit. Every time I looked up, there was some chick in his face. Everywhere we went, he had a bitch there. I was growing tired of it.

It was something about this chick I could tell he liked because the nigga didn't even acknowledge me. Last chick that had gotten killed, nigga introduced me as his girl, but here it is today, I get hit with a fucking head nod.

The constant ringing of my phone made me look down. Noticing it was Mari, I let it go to voicemail. Right now, I didn't want anything to do with anybody that was associated with Cali. As soon as my phone stopped ringing, it rang again, but this time it was Cali. I sent his ass to voicemail and he called back over and over until I powered my phone off.

Making it a few miles from the mall, I headed over to Brick's house. I needed some weed and I was gonna fuck the shit out his sexy ass to get my mind off Calhoun. Brick and I had met about four months ago. I gave him my number and all we did was talk on the phone at first. One day, I saw him in the neighborhood and he told me he was looking for a spot to open. Not knowing he was a Dope Boy, I finally felt comfortable with telling him what I did for a living. Thank God I did, because I started copping from him at a cheaper price and better product. After that, Brick and I chilled a few times, but we never fucked.

As bad as I wanted to surrender myself to him, I couldn't. Just like Cali, I knew It was a possibility of me falling for Brick, so I kept my distance. The difference between the two, was, Cali demanded my attention while Brick played shit cool. He never pressed me to go out, but he did call me every day. I hadn't talked to him since the other day when Cali hung up on him, so I was kinda embarrassed to show up. But fuck it, I needed him right now. Or did I?

"Knock, knock, knock." I banged on his door and waited for him to answer.

I waited for a few seconds before I turned to walk away. Right when I made it down the stairs, the door flew open. A chick walked out with her hair all over the place like she had just got the life fucked out of her. Brick stood on the porch shirtless and I couldn't do shit but admire his body. This man was sexy as hell.

"I'm sorry I didn't..."

"You good." He licked his lips. The girl mugged me, but I tried my best to ignore her. I wasn't here for that today, but I swear if she wanted it she could get it; especially how I was feeling.

"I just wanted a bag."

"Hold up," he said, then walked into the house.

He came back moments later and handed me the bag of weed. When I tried to pull my money out, he told me don't trip. Seeing the chick wasn't gonna leave, I turned to leave deciding to catch an Uber home. I couldn't win for losing with these niggas today. All I wanted to do was go home and lay in my bed.

"Dreu, it's a guy at the door for you?" my granny shook me to wake me up.

I groggily climbed out my bed because it couldn't be anybody but Kojak. He was the only one brave enough to come to my door. I went into my restroom and rinsed my mouth with mouthwash then headed to the front. When I opened my door, my face instantly frowned up seeing that it was Cali. He was on a royal blue and red dirt bike and he held his helmet in his hand.

How the fuck he know where I stay? Kaloni. Ohh I'mma kick her ass. I thought as I watched him.

"Come here," he told me, but my body stood frozen. I was caught up with being upset and mesmerized at the same time. This man was so sexy it was hard for me to resist him. I swear I felt like Eve staring at that shiny ass apple. I let out a soft sigh then made my way down the porch stairs before my nosey ass granny came back out the room.

"What, Anthony?"

"Anthony?" he asked with a chuckle.

"Man, what you want?"

"Why yo phone off?"

"Why do you care?" I asked as I folded my arms across each

other. I tried so hard to be tough, but I swear I wanted to just cry in front this nigga.

"I don't get you, Dreu. You keep telling me you don't want a nigga, but then you trip when you see me with a bitch. You confusing the fuck out of me yo," he said, shaking his head.

"Dee, let me get a dime." Kojak walked up and whispered into my ear.

"Around the corner." I quickly, replied hoping Cali didn't hear him. He looked at us, but I guess he did, because he hit Kojak with a head nod then focused back on me.

"So, what the fuck is it gone be because a nigga ain't got time for yo little games."

"I'm not playing games with you."

"Man, you really a little ass girl," he said, putting on his helmet. He started his bike and took one last look at me. Shaking his head, he pulled off and left me standing there. This time I couldn't hold the tears back. They fell from my eyes freely.

After standing in one spot hoping Cali would come back, the nigga never did. I decided to head to Ms. Brenda's house because I needed to make some money. I needed an outfit for this block party Mari mentioned because I was going to show up and show out.

When I made it to my spot, I noticed a nigga standing on the corner serving someone. I had never seen this nigga before and he had me all the way fucked up. I walked over to him and stood in his face.

"What the fuck you doing?" I asked in a rage.

"Mind yo fucking business," he said like I wasn't shit.

"Nigga this is my fucking business. You got five minutes to get the fuck from right here or shit gonna get ugly."

"Bitch you ain't gone do shit," he said walking closer to me.

I guess today really wasn't my day. I looked up at the sky then down to my watch. I had about a good hour before the sun went completely down. I shot him one last look then walked into the spot.

"Ms. Brenda, you know that nigga?"

"No, honey, but he been there all day. He was here yesterday, too. I called you, but you didn't answer."

"Okay," was all I said

. I went into the room that I spent most of my time in and fumbled through the clothing I had scattered out. I pulled out some black sweats and a black tee. The tee had writing on the front, so I turned it inside out. I slid into the clothes then went into the living room and took a seat. I pulled out my sack and counted out a few grams to give Ms. Brenda. The grams would hold me over for about two days. Ms. Brenda didn't charge me rent, she wanted her money in work. I didn't have a problem with it, especially for the price I was paying.

I sat in the chair for close to an hour and I haven't made one sell. When I looked out the window, just like I said, the sun had went down and it was now show time. I crept out the back door and hopped the gate that led to a house on the next block. I jogged up the street and came back around to the corner. From where I stood, I could see the guy still on the corner. He had his back to me and that was perfect. I crept up on him and I guess he heard my footsteps because he quickly turned around.

"You still here, huh?" he asked unmoved by my presence.

"I thought I told you to leave?"

"Bitch and I told you mind yo business."

I reached into the pockets of my sweats and pulled out my 38. His eyes grew wide, but he tried to act hard like he wasn't moved.

"Fuck you gon' do with that little shit?" he said, taunting me.

See this was the problem with men. They were naive as hell when it came to women. They thought we couldn't do shit, but be cute and pregnant, but what this nigga didn't know; I wasn't the average woman.

"I'm telling you nigga, either you leave from my corner or leave to meet your maker."

The nigga laughed in my face like I wasn't shit. Growing tired of this nigga, I lifted my gun and fired a shot into his stomach. He fell back falling smack dead into a car. I sent another two shots into his upper body and as soon as I went to finish him off, my damn gun jammed. I pulled the trigger again and again, but it was stuck. I watched as his body slid down from the car to the ground as I still tried my gun.

"Bit...you stupid bitch..." he said trying his best to speak.

"I guess it's your lucky day," I said then kicked him in the head.

Hoping no one noticed me, I turned around and jogged up the block. I cut through a back house then jumped a gate to get across another gate. I landed in the yard I needed to get to Ms. Brenda's backyard. When I hopped the gate, Ms. Brenda was already at the back door waiting for me.

"Chile get yo ass in here," she said, shoving me into the home. "Change your clothes and go home. Don't come back for a few days Dee, shit gone be hot around here."

Without replying, I shook my head yes. I went into the room and changed back into my clothing. I was gonna listen to Ms. Brenda and duck off. I knew the police were gonna be swarming the area because the police station wasn't too far. I couldn't risk going to jail because my grandma and Micah needed me. I hated I had to do this today, but I needed to make a statement. Apparently, these niggas knew the area belonged to somebody because they sent the nigga to shortstop. I hope the nigga took it as a message and decided to leave my shit alone. I didn't bother anyone and I didn't step on no toes. So fuck em!

TEN

Calhoun

"So, you mean to tell me you let a bitch get up on you my nigga?"

"Yeah, shit she came out of nowhere."

"So, what she say?"

"I told her mind her fucking business and she said this was her business. She pulled out a strap and started shooting."

"My nigga where was yo fucking strap?"

"It was in the car. I had to leave it in the car because the ones is hot right there."

I shook my head at this dumb ass nigga. He got exactly what the fuck he deserved. I stood to my feet and tossed the nigga the duffle bag that contained twenty gee's in it.

"That's for your hospital bill and some extra change. When you get out this hospital, your services is no longer needed," I told him and turned to head out.

"What you mean? You acting like this shit my fault."

I turned around to grill the nigga. I swear I wanted to just empty my whole clip on his dumb ass but because he was laying in this hospital, I chose against it.

"You heard what the fuck I said," was all I said.

There was nothing else to be said. I didn't need no weak ass niggas in my camp. This nigga let somebody creep up on him and shoot his damn ass and not to mention, he had a strap. For now, I was gonna let the nigga breathe, but I swear the minute he got out, I was gonna finish the job.

I exited the hospital and hopped in my car. I drove to my crib out in West, so I could jump in my truck and head out to the block party. I was driving the truck today because I was pulling my bikes on the back. I wasn't gonna let this shit with Pete fuck up my day. I was gonna turn the fuck up at the party and tear the streets up on my bikes.

Every year, East and I had these parties for the community. We did giveaways for kids, we raffled off bikes and toys and we even had jumpers down the whole block. The parties were set up in front of my trap spot on the westside, but today, we were setting up on the East in front the spot we had just opened a few months ago.

I got issues, yeah I got problems with commitment baby
I apologized to you I should've listened baby
I wasn't in love with them hoes, I was just pimping baby
I knew my part, knew my role, I wasn't slippin baby

Pulling up to the party two hours after it started, y'all know a nigga had to make a grand entrance. Every bitch from California was in attendance, so I had many hoes to choose from. After the bullshit Dreu was taking me through, I decided to give up on baby girl and do me. I was done trying with her childish ass. I mean, she had all rights to be upset seeing me with Jazzy, but what the fuck was I supposed to do? No matter how much I tried to show her, no matter how good I dicked her down, her ass still always hit me with the *I don't want a relationship* shit. This girl was confused as fuck, but fuck that, she could be confused by her damn self.

I hopped out my truck and called a smoker over by the name Leon so he could bring my bikes down. Bitches were chattering and niggas were staring, but I ignored everybody. Half these niggas I didn't know, so to me they were groupies. Shit, I didn't know half the bitches here either, but they made it their business to show up. Knowing I was looking good, I walked through the crowd to find East. I was rocking my black jeans and a custom dirt bike shirt that read Calhoun and matched my bike. I had my goggles on my head that matched my shirt and a pair of red and white 12's on my feet to match. Today, I only wore one chain, which was my gold rope that held my oversized Jesus piece. I had on my Jesus piece earrings I just copped because fucking with Dreu, I had lost one.

"Calhoun!" my name was being called from all angles. I slapped hands with a couple people as I made my way through the crowd. I walked over to East who was standing there with three chicks and Benji.

"Hey, Calhoun," one girl said, smiling. I hit her with a head nod and focused my attention on East and Benji.

"You just left the hospital?" East asked.

"Yeah, man," I said, shaking my head. He didn't say much because these random chicks were right here, and I couldn't wait to tell this nigga what Pete had told me. "Aye, you get that dough up there to Chef Neecee?"

"Yeah, that's handled." I shook my head in agreeance.

I had sent twenty bands up to *Kan I get a Plate* for what happened the other day. That's just the type of nigga I was. I wanted to slide Frenisha moms some dough to cover her service, but I didn't need them questioning me.

"Who you put on the grill? A nigga starving," I asked East.

"I got Lenard and Mama Fee cooking."

"Oh, hell yeah," I said, rubbing my stomach.

Mama Fee got down. She sold plates out her crib every Sunday and believe me I was always there. Because I didn't have my parents, I missed out on a lot of home cooked meals. I guess that's why I wanted Dreu. I was hoping she would be more of a lady and get her ass in the kitchen for a nigga.

"Aye, make me a plate. And if you poison my shit I'mma kill you," I told one of the chicks that was standing with East when I first walked up.

Instead of the chick objecting, she giggled and walked over to the grill. She tried to switch her little ass as hard as she could, but I ignored her. She wasn't cute at all and she ain't have no ass.

"Bitch ain't got no ass," East started laughing.

"And her friend look like a pterodactyl. Where you get them bitches?" I frowned up.

"Man them Benji bitches." I looked over at Benji.

"Man they got some good pussy."

"They?" I asked and me and East fell out laughing.

"Man don't tell me you invited Kaloni" I looked at East stupid ass.

"Nah, I didn't invite her. I don't know how the fuck she knew about this event."

Dreu was wearing a short ass dress that was too short for my liking. They walked over to us and Kaloni wrapped her arms around East then looked at me to say hi. I hit her with a head nod then turned my attention elsewhere.

"Here's your plate." Ol girl walked up, making Dreu frown up.

To my surprise she didn't say shit, which was good. I walked over to a table that sat way across from where they stood. I sat down and began to eat my food. I wanted to be far away from that childish ass girl.

"Hey, Calhoun." I turned around to see who was it that took it upon them self to sit down.

"Thing 1...I mean..."

"Kamika," she corrected me.

"What's up ma?" I chuckled to myself.

"How you been?" she asked, making small talk.

"I been good. What's up with you? Where Thing 2?" I asked, laughing.

"She's over there with your friend." I looked in the direction she was talking about and noticed her friend talking to Jock. When I turned back around, Dreu was mugging me from across the room. I dropped my head laughing inside. I took a spoon of the potato salad that ol girl had piled on my plate wishing Kamika would get up and leave.

"Let me go before yo boo come tripping," she said looking at Dreu. When I looked in her direction, she smirked. I shook my head. I watched her in her short ass dress as she took a sip of her drink.

Who the fuck gave her liquor? I thought knowing once she got drunk it was gonna be some shit.

I finished eating my food then headed over to my bike. I climbed on then cranked it up. As soon as it started, I revved the gas. I dropped it in neutral and slowly backed up. Once I found my lane to ride in, I dropped down to first and pulled off. Once I got a good speed, I kicked up to third and went flying. As soon as I got to the corner, I made a U and took off again. Of course, I was gonna show off, so I played with my back brake and hit a wheelie all the way up the block. All eyes were on me like always. I did this a few times then pulled alongside the curb. When I pulled up, I noticed Dreu all up in some nigga's face. My blood instantly began to boil. I wanted so bad to go snatch her ass up, but I had to remind myself she wasn't my bitch.

"Can I ride with you?" I turned around and got the shock of my life.

"What's up, Yanna." I smiled at Ayanna, who stood there looking good as fuck. I hadn't seen her in years, but nothing had changed. I could tell she still kept herself up.

"Hey stranger," she said, smiling showing off her pretty ass teeth.

Ayanna was a chick I used to smash before I went to jail. Out of all the bitches, she was the only one I didn't hold a grudge against for leaving me.

Ayanna was a Pediatrician and she wasn't built for no nigga like me. I guess she got a thrill out of fucking with a hood nigga, so we fucked with each other heavy. Out of all my bitches, Ayanna was the one I would have wifed. Not only was she beautiful, but she had her head on straight. However, she didn't give me a chance because she had her mind made up on going to school and I went to jail.

"Hop on," I told her, then hit her with my smile. She always told me she loved my dimple, so I used that shit as my weapon.

"Don't make me fall boy?"

"You know I got you ma," I told her, starting up the bike.

She wrapped her arms around my waist tight and the scent of her perfume hit me. *Damn I missed her ass;* I thought as we went flying down the street.

ELEVEN

Dreu

I watched as Cali rode up and down the streets showing off doing wheelies. He looked so damn good. I was kinda jealous. It's like every bitch at this entire party was lusting over him. Every nigga in the crowd wanted to be him. East wasn't no damn angel either because since we had been standing here, all types of bitches came up to him. Out of respect for Kaloni, he brushed them off. Unlike Cali, that nigga kept a bitch in his face every time he moved. Like right now, the nigga acted like I didn't exist, but I had something for him. I spotted Brick who was a few feet away. I walked over to him and covered his eyes with my hands. When he turned around, he was smiling.

"Sup ma?"

"Hey, Brick." I blushed.

"You leaving with me?" he said grabbing my hand.

"I ain't gotta beat a bitch up, do I?" I played it off and pulled away from him. I wasn't that damn crazy. Cali would shoot this party up with no remorse.

"Nah, you good," he laughed.

"I guess so," I smiled at his sexy ass. Brick was a sexy chocolate with pearly white teeth. He stood about six feet and had a body to die for. "What you doing here anyway?"

"Shit my people dragged me to this shit."

"Oh, okay."

Brick continued to talk to me, but something more interesting caught my attention. Cali had some chick all in his face. The way he was smiling let me know it was personal. I instantly became jealous.

"Oh, this nigga got me fucked up," I said to myself, but out loud.

Brick looked in the direction I was looking and smirked. It was something about the way he smirked that puzzled me, but I left it alone.

I stormed over to where Cali and ol girl had just pulled from. He had pulled off with her on the back of his bike. I patiently waited for him to roll back up because I was about to fight his ass right here in front of everybody.

"Un un, Dreu," Kaloni said, walking up on me.

"No, Loni, this nigga got me fucked up," I said on a verge of crying. I was drunk as hell, so I was really in my feelings.

I stomped away from her as I saw Cali's bike pull up down the street. He wasn't even paying me any mind because he was too busy giggling with his little bitch.

"What's up, Cali?" I spoke with so much hatred. He slowly turned around like he was annoyed with my presence.

"Sup," was all he said.

"I'm gonna head over to my car. Thanks, Anthony, I'll see you soon."

"Anthony?" I frowned. "Nah baby girl, you won't be seeing him," I spat.

The chick smirked like shit was funny. I went to walk up in her face and I swear this nigga jumped up so fast his bike hit the ground hard, making everyone look in our direction. He shoved me so hard, I fell to the ground. Whoever this chick was, he was protecting her. I was so embarrassed tears began to pour from my eyes. The chick walked off like she had won, and that shit hurt my feelings more.

"My bad, I didn't mean...."

"Get the fuck away from me hoe!" I shouted to the top of my lungs.

I was gonna embarrass him just like he had done me. I knew he wasn't used to nobody talking to him like this so guess what, I was gonna show the world I wasn't scared of Calhoun.

I stormed up the street with Cali on my heels. I was gone turn up the block and just walk to my trap spot that wasn't far, but I couldn't risk him knowing what I did. Kojak dumb ass had already almost given me up.

"Man, slow yo ass down!" Cali shouted, snatching my arm back.

I snatched away from him and slapped the shit out of him. He grabbed my arm and twisted it behind my back. He shoved me into a gate and up the stairs. Using his free hand, he opened the door and pushed me inside.

"Everybody get the fuck out," he shouted, and everyone scattered. "Man bring yo dumb ass here," he said shoving me into a room. The room was much cleaner than the rest of the house. I assumed this was one of Cali's spot. Fear had taken over me because if this was his spot, then that meant I was his competition.

Oh boy.

"Didn't I tell you about putting yo fucking hands on me."

"Nigga, you embarrassed me in front of all those people."

"I embarrassed you? Dreu, you had a nigga all up in yo fucking face and in front of my fucking peoples. Brah you need to make up yo fucking mind on what you wanna do. One minute you want a nigga, then next you don't want me. Make up yo fucking mind."

"I just don't wanna get hurt! I don't want you to hurt me, Anthony!" I started swinging on him as I burst out into tears. This nigga was bringing a side of me out I never knew I had. I was a G. Couldn't no nigga make me cry, or so I thought.

"I'm not gonna hurt you ma," he said, grabbing my hands.

He pulled me close to him and kissed me. I was so defeated; I accepted the kiss. My heart was beating fast and I was breathing hard. Things began to get hot and next thing I knew, he was snatching my dress off. *Thank god I wore panties.*

Cali stepped out of his shoes followed by his jeans. He flung his goggles across the room, then took his shirt off. His dick was standing at attention, making my mouth water. I never gave head in my life, but I wanted so bad to lick his. It was beautiful. Without warning, he forcefully bent me over and rammed himself inside of me making me gasp.

"Ohhhh shit!" I was panting. "Fuuuuck baby you hurting me."

"So what, take this shit," he said and continued to stroke me hard.

Not one to submit, I threw my ass back, making it clap against his legs.

"That's right baby. Fuck yo dick," he said, and that shit made me throw it back harder. He began to bite my neck and I knew I was gonna have a hickey.

"Ohhhh, shit daddy," I called out not meaning to.

"I'm daddy, now baby?" he was still stroking.

"Yes daddy!"

"So, you mine now? Huh?"

"Yes ...ahhh yes. I'm yours, Calhoun." It was like that was all he needed to hear.

He slowed down his pace and started kissing me all over my neck. I could feel my liquids flowing down my legs. This nigga dick was magical. His shit was hand carved by God himself and it was made just for me. As he went in and out, I could feel my walls clamp down locking him in. I was in pure bliss.

We went at it for about another thirty minutes until I felt his dick grow harder and pulsating inside of me. Next thing I know, he released every last drop inside of me. He was now growling as he held on to me for dear life. Again, I began to climax until my knees became weak. We stood there in the same spot relishing the moment. I didn't want this man to let me go ever. I had my hands on his arms holding him near me. He kissed my neck then broke free. He was still naked, but he walked out the door. When he walked back into the room, he was holding a towel. He tossed it to me and began to dress himself. After I washed up, I slid my dress over my head.

"I should beat yo ass for that little ass dress," he said eyeing me, but I ignored him.

We walked out the room hand and hand and everything felt different at this moment. When we stepped off the porch, I stopped and took a long hard sigh. I looked at Cali and he smiled at me for assurance. I squeezed his hand tight and he did the same. That's all I needed. We headed back over to where everyone stood, and they all looked at us like we were crazy. I was in la la land and I guess Cali was too because he couldn't take his eyes off me.

The fellas stood to the side as Kaloni and I gossiped on the sideline. I couldn't stop smiling as my insides cringed.

"So, is it official?" Kaloni asked.

I guess she could sense something was different because Cali and I couldn't keep our eyes or hands off each other. Every few minutes, he came over and kissed me. I had never been public with a man, so I was shy as hell. Because I knew every woman here wanted him, it made me blush even more.

"I guess."

"What you mean you guess? Bitch the way y'all acting and judging by those hickeys on yo neck yeah y'all official," Kaloni smirked.

"Yes, we're official."

"Yayyy. Oh, my, God I knew it," she clapped her hands making me laugh.

"Hey y'all," Mari walked up smiling from ear to ear.

I looked down at her shorts and I knew all hell was about to break loose. I looked over at Cali and he was already grilling her. I looked away from him and dropped my head. I didn't want any parts of this shit.

"Girl you trying to get us killed." I looked at Mari like she was crazy. When I saw Cali walking our way, I pulled her and Kaloni away and pretended we were gonna get food.

"Bring y'all ass here," Cali said, making us all stop.

"Because I'm in a good mood I'm not gone trip, but don't make that shit no habit." He looked down at Mari's shorts. I sighed out in relief. "Where the fuck y'all going anyway?" he asked, pulling me back.

"Babyyy," I whined like a child. Kaloni was giggling and Mari was smirking.

"We're going to get food. You hungry?"

"Nah, I'm straight."

"Yeah, I forgot one of yo little groupies made yo plate."

"Don't start yo shit ma."

"Dreu, you ready to roll?" I turned to look over and Brick stood there wearing a smirk.

I couldn't say shit because I was caught off guard. I could tell by the look her wore he knew what he was doing. Before I could check him, Cali stepped up.

"Nigga she ain't going nowhere with you." I was now shitting bricks because I knew what both men are capable of. Brick wasn't no bitch and Cali for sure wasn't. I had to step in so things wouldn't get ugly.

"Baby lets go." I tried to pull Cali's arm, but he shoved me away. "Don't do that, Brick." I mugged his ass hard. I was pissed the fuck off because I didn't do that shit to him when his little bitch was over. I got my weed and left peacefully.

"What I'm doing? You told me you were leaving with me," Brick said, laughing. Before I knew it, Cali had whipped out his gun and was about to kill this nigga right here. Brick didn't back down and Cali wasn't playing.

"Please baby. It's a million people out here," I whispered into his ear. I swear he looked like the devil himself.

"Please listen to her, Cali," Mari pleaded.

I turned around and about twelve men stood behind Cali with their guns out.

Oh lord. I thought as I looked around at all the men.

Brick had brought this shit on himself. However, I prayed Cali would hear me out. There were too many witnesses and believe, everyone looked on. Mothers started grabbing their babies and ran with them close to them. This wasn't a good look for Cali and all I could do was look around.

When Brick threw his hands up in surrender, I closed my eyes and let out a sigh. This nigga didn't stand a chance and I guess he knew it. What I also knew was, this shit was far from over. I just prayed Cali made it out on top.

TWELVE

East

---

*A*s Cali and I drove out to my crib I shared with Jen, we chopped it up about this nigga who name I now knew as Brick. I wanted that nigga head so bad I could taste that nigga blood. He had violated my brother by even testing my nigga. I had never seen this nigga in my life, but upon doing my homework, I heard he was pushing major weight. Cali asked Dreu a million fucking times was she fucking with the nigga and she swore she wasn't. It was something about the way she looked at him when he said he was gonna kill the nigga.

"I couldn't believe she had told that nigga she was gonna roll out with him. No matter what the fuck was going on, she was gonna stoop that low to go fuck with a nigga." He shook his head then looked out the window. "On my mama, I'mma kill that nigga."

"I already know man." I couldn't do shit but shake my head.

"Keep a close eye on the nigga, East, but don't kill him. I want that nigga to myself."

"I got you bro. And I got Jacob digging up everything he can on the nigga"

Jacob was my little brother, who I kept out the streets. He was a straight A college student and worked as a Software Developer. This nigga was smart as hell when it came to computers. He was the one who ran our accounts and handled our business. So aside from his career, we paid him great. Jacob is three years younger than me, but he acted like he was my big brother. My moms spoiled the nigga to death, so he really didn't need for shit.

"So, you not taking her with us?" I asked him, referring to Dreu.

"Why because you taking Kaloni, huh?" he smirked.

"Hell yeah. Nigga I gotta get all the time in I could. Shit sooner or later, Jenn ain't having that shit."

"Man, Jenny from the block gone kill yo ass." We both laughed. This nigga had been calling her that since he met her.

"She mad at me, too."

"Fuck you do?"

"She was talking shit. so I took the argument further just so I could stay with Kaloni." The nigga fell out laughing.

"Nigga you really like that chick."

"Yeah, I ain't gone lie." I was truthful. "Ahh nigga, I didn't tell you what happened? Why we was fucking and her moms came in the room."

"She caught y'all fucking?"

"Hell yeah."

"So what the fuck you do?"

"I got my ass up. Then gave her some crack." I turned to look away from Cali.

"Nigga ain't you the same captain save a hoe ass nigga that told all our workers not to serve her." He was still laughing.

"Yeah, I fucked up."

"Well, shit, Butter gone feed her the shit anyway. Nigga keep her in there getting his dick sucked." We both fell out laughing. Shit wasn't funny, but the way Cali said it and his facial expression he made had a nigga dying.

Fuck her ass at? I thought as we pulled into my driveway.

Cali and I headed into the house. Since Jenn wasn't here, I was gonna hurry and pack my shit for our trip. We were about to fly out to Mexico to holla at our connect. We had these meetings every month and it was the perfect chance for Kaloni and I to get away.

"Why you moving so fast?" Cali asked, laughing.

"Nigga I'm trying to hurry before Jenn muthafuckin' ass come back. Her ass be..." Before I could finish, Cali dumb ass was pointing, which let me know Jenn was standing right behind me.

When I turned around, she had her arms folded over one another.

"Sup baby?" I smiled, trying hard to hold my laugh.

"Don't what's up baby me." she rolled her eyes.

"Come here girl stop tripping."

"Nah, I'm good," she said, walking past me. I walked back into the room behind her. I needed to break the ice, so I could have a clear mind when I took this trip.

When I walked into the room, Jenn was digging through the drawer and pulled out her night clothes. I looked at my Rolex because it was only 6:30 pm and her ass never went to sleep this early. She then walked into the restroom and began running the shower.

"Where you bout to go?" I asked her, as she walked back and forth from the restroom and the room. She was giving me the silent treatment and that shit was about to annoy me.

"You don't hear me talking to you?" I pulled her arm.

"I'm not going anywhere I just need to wash my ass."

"And why is that what you been doing today?"

"I ain't been doing shit. I had this on yesterday."

"Yesterday?" I looked at her like she was crazy. "So that mean you ain't come home last night."

"Did you come home last night?" she shot, smartly.

"But I was handling business the fuck was you doing?"

"I was with Gina."

"So, you was with that hoe?"

"And you was with that hoe in there?" she shot, then walked into the restroom.

I stood there for some time looking stupid as fuck. She was playing mind games with a nigga and that shit wasn't cool. I walked over to the bed and grabbed my duffle bag. I was gonna deal with her ass when I got back. I knew what I had to do and that was wine and dine her. I had been neglecting the fuck out of her, so I knew all she wanted was attention, but right now I couldn't give it to her. Like I said, I needed a clear mind for this trip. I walked back into the living room Cali was on the phone, so I motioned for him to get up, so we could roll. He already knew what was up because he knew Jenn stayed tripping.

When we got into the car, I grabbed my phone from the cup holder. I called Kaloni just as I was pulling out the driveway. When I turned to pull out, I felt someone watching me. I looked at the house and Jennifer was in the window. She wore a sad ass look that made me feel bad as fuck. I wanted so bad to turn around and say fuck this trip, but business came first.

"Helloooo," I heard Kaloni's voice on the other end of the phone.

"My bad. You ready?"

"By the time you get here, I will be. Where you at anyway? I been calling you."

"Is Dreu ready?" I asked, changing the subject.

I tried not to look at Cali who was mugging the fuck out me from the passenger's side. Because of the smirk I wore, he knew what I was up to.

"Yeah she's right here."

"Aight well we on our way."

"Okay."

When we pulled up to Kaloni's crib, her mom was sitting on the porch with another lady who looked just as strung out as she was.

Cali and I exited the car and walked straight in before Pearl got a chance to beg. She was using me and Loni getting caught as her ammo. Out of guilt, I fed her habit every chance I got. I hoped like hell Loni would never find out, but my gut told me it was only a matter of time.

"Man y'all need to bring y'all ass on."

"We ready, but Dreu need to grab some stuff."

Cali looked at Dreu and rolled his eyes at her like a little bitch. I couldn't do shit but laugh. She caught it and did the same.

Reaching down, I grabbed Kaloni's bag. I guess Dreu thought Cali was gonna do the same, but that nigga kept it pushing right out the door. She smacked her lips and grabbed her own bag. When we got to the car, I turned around to Kaloni.

"Aye ma you put that money up right?" I asked, making sure.

"Yes, baby for the one hundredth time."

"Just making sure," I replied and climbed into the car.

I had giving Kaloni 20 bands to put up. Really it wasn't for me, it was for her whenever she needed something. I didn't tell her because I knew she would decline. I looked down at my phone and shot Drak a text that we were on the way. We had a nice long trip and a nigga was ready. We were about to up our product, which was gonna be a big move for us.

THIRTEEN

Calhoun

_____

$\mathcal{W}$e pulled up to the Slauson Swap meet because Dreu's little hood ass chose to come here. If it was up to me, baby could have been on Melrose, but I wasn't fucking with her like that right now. You damn right, I was still salty about that shit with that nigga Brick. Just when baby girl and I finally decided to give this shit a shot, she do some hoe ass shit. I mean I understand it was before we had made up, but damn, she was really gonna leave with the nigga. Straight hoe shit.

As I walked through the swap meet, I saw a few blood niggas I knew from the East Side. When I say these niggas was flamed up in red shirts and red chuck Taylors, they could be spotted a mile away. See a nigga like me had love all over Cali. I was respected by bloods and crips because I was a real nigga. Gangbanging wasn't never in me because I was a Trap God and in this world, it was you either banging or balling.

I slapped hands with my boy T Spoon out the Bottoms. Spoon was a cool nigga I was locked up with in Delano. We programmed together, and the nigga helped my time go by faster. He had looked over my paperwork and even helped me on my case. I was looking at fourteen years, but ended up doing foe with half thanks to him. After hollering at Spoon, I went to holla at my boy Alex at the jewelry booth. I had a couple pieces he had made for me and even Jazzy. Right now, I was just gonna get my shit cleaned then go buy some socks and a couple white tees. I was ready to roll so I hopped like hell Dreu ass hurried up. I didn't even understand why was she coming with us anyway. This was business and her or Kaloni didn't need to tag along.

After we were done in the Slauson, we headed for the airport. Our flight was due to leave in an hour, so we were slightly rushing. Thanks to Dreu, who spent hours in a damn swap meet on bullshit, we were damn near late. I sat in the airport chair watching her as she walked over to McDonalds. She was looking sexy as hell in a long grey lounge dress. With every step, her ass clapped giving her an instant murphy. I ain't gon front, she had a nigga dick hard as fuck. When she turned around, I tried to hurry up and turn my head, but I knew I was caught. She smirked at me and continued on her mission. I laid back in my seat and waited to board the flight. I couldn't wait to get to Mexico because I was gonna get some fire ass head from one of those Hispanic chicks Drak kept around him.

Ayanna: *Hey stranger.*
I looked down and saw text from Ayanna. I couldn't even help the smile that crept up on my face.
Me: *Sup baby?*
Ayanna: *Lol wyd*
Me: *out the way right now...can I take you out when I get back?"*
Ayanna: *Idk Anthony (sus face)*
Me: *Girl I'll be there to pick you up. Send me your address.*
Ayanna: *Lol okay*

I actually text Ayanna damn near my entire flight. She had a nigga laughing and of course, I could tell Dreu was getting upset. I wasn't tripping off her right now because she was foul in my eyes. When I got back to the city, I was gonna scoop Ayanna up and see where shit would go from there. I really liked Yanna back in the day and it was like looking at her brought back those old feelings. She was still sexy as fuck and even cool to talk to. That girl had her head on her shoulders and this is what a nigga like me needed. Fucking with a chick like Dreu was challenging and I had enough shit going on in my life. Now Ayanna on the other hand, was the type of chick who would stay home pregnant and cooking for a nigga. She had her own bread so I didn't have to worry bout no gold digger bullshit with her. Not saying Dreu was a gold digger, but she sat around on her ass all day. I asked her before was she gonna ever go to school or get a job and all she did was shrug her shoulders. She kept money, so I assumed she got some type of assistance. She wasn't rolling in dough, but she was well off from what I could see.

∼

"I just don't understand why the fuck they had to come." I shot at East as we pulled up to Drak's home.

"Because we didn't have time to take them to the hotel. Man, you already know how this nigga is when we late. Chill bro we in and out. Then y'all could go fight while me and my baby fuck until the sun come up," he said making Kaloni turn beat red.

"I ain't fucking with this Skank."

"Fuck you, Anthony. I'm tired of yo shit," she said upset.

Ever since Mari called me by my government in the mall, she had been hitting me with it frequently.

"Don't call me that. You ain't got that privilege no more."

"Whatever," she said, rolling her eyes, but I was serious.

"Man lets go," East said, hopping out the whip.

I climbed out behind him followed by the girls. We headed to Drak's door and was let in on the second knock. I didn't understand why we had to go through all this when they already had to buzz us in the fucking gate.

"Calhoun, East. what's up," Drak said the moment we entered the room.

"Sup Papi chulo," I said, laughing.

Drak was one of those pretty niggas with the hair. He was mixed with Mexican and black due to his pops being full blood Mexican. His moms was full black and a fucking gangsta. Drak's pops Gizmo had stepped down a few years back and that's when Drak stepped up. My pops and Gizmo did business back in the days, which is how Gizmo knew exactly who I was when they approached me. The areas I had now on the eastside was passed to me from Drak. His boys couldn't handle the area due to gang violence, so I took over. I wasn't worried bout no gang shit because like I said, I proved that I wasn't to be fucked with. I had enough money and guns to wipe out a nigga whole hood.

"You the chulo nigga," he laughed and stood from behind his desk.

He looked at Kaloni and hit her with a head nod. When his eyes fell onto Dreu, the nigga stopped and took in her appearance. I don't know if I was tripping or not, but she was lusting over the nigga too.

"Let's get this show on the road," East said peeping the shit too.

"Oh...yeah...my bad." Drak laughed out, but he couldn't take his eyes off Dreu.

I could tell now she was uncomfortable because she dropped her head and started playing with her phone. This was something she did whenever she was nervous. Shit had me 38 hot, ready to whip my strap out and kill both they ass. On my Daddy, if I knew I'd make it out alive, I probably would have, but this nigga had guards all over this bitch and right now Dreu wasn't worth my life.

"You guys ready to go into the private room?" Drak asked us.

"Hell yeah," I said, anxiously.

"Let's roll," he said, and we followed suit.

East had explained to the girls they couldn't go inside so they remained seated. East and I followed Drak into what he called the private room. When we walked in, I already had my eyes set on a pretty ass chick with hair past her ass. See these days even Hispanic chicks had ass, or they were getting ass shots. Whatever the case might be, baby girl was bad hands down.

"I see you got your eyes set on, Angel."

"Yeah, she bad as fuck." I rubbed my hands together.

"Angel, Selena, come here."

When they walked over to us, I noticed Angel was even prettier up close. I grabbed Angel's hand and the Selena chick was sent to get us liquor. Drak hit the button on his lights and the entire room turned into a nightclub setting. Stripper poles came down from in the ceiling and the music began to play. East walked over to the bar like he always did, and me, I took Angel over to the pole and made her climb that muthafucka. I wanted a show. then after, I'd get some head and bounce. We always discussed business as we got pleasure. This shit was a normal routine. I mean why not make the best of this shit while we were in town? Shit we were here for three days and Dreu wasn't on my best list at the moment.

Dreu

When we walked into Drak's crib, I expected it to be some old Mexican man in an expensive suit with grey hair, but no. Instead, I was met with the most handsome man I'd ever laid eyes on. Now don't get me wrong, Cali was fine as fuck, too. See, Cali was rough around the edges and cocky like I liked them, but Drak, he looked well groomed, and respectable. He had a pretty bronze skin tone and a pair mysterious eyes to die for. His built was masculine and he had long silky hair that I imagined myself running my fingers through. This nigga looked like one of those sexy men that would play Tarzan or Conan in a movie. His lips were full, and his smile was the pretties I'd ever seen. Keep it one hundred, he wasn't my type at all, but a girl could flirt and fantasize right?

Right now, I was caught up in Cali's web. I saw no man on this earth besides him. This nigga had my head gone no matter how hard I tried to act. He was still tripping over Brick after I explained to him why I did what I did. This nigga hadn't talked to me since the day of that block party and every day, I died inside. And again, he made me realize exactly why I didn't want to be in love. I didn't want a man to come in and invade my mind, body and soul. This nigga Cali had a hex on me and couldn't nobody tell me any different.

"They been in there for a long ass time," I said, getting annoyed.

"Do you think they're okay?" Kaloni responded, nervously.

"Girl you watch too many damn movies," I laughed.

Right then, Cali and East walked out of a door to the private room. I stood up, immediately because I was ready to go. Drak's eyes fell onto mines and I felt uneasy. Cali peeped game because he grilled me.

"I'll see you guys soon," Drak said, but never taking his eyes off me.

"Eyes over here nigga," Cali said.

"Yes, my bad." Drak said then looked over to the fellas.

As we headed towards the door, I could feel his eyes watching me. I tried not to look, but I couldn't help it. I turned to look at him one last time and our eyes met again. I quickly turned my head because I could feel Cali watching us. The moment we stepped out of the home, I let out the deep breath I had been holding since first laying eyes on Drak. We went to the car and everybody got in. I couldn't wait to get to the hotel because I wanted to shower and relax. We had a hotel on the beach and because this was my first time in Mexico, I was gonna take advantage.

When we got to our hotel, we checked in and got on the elevator to go up. When we made it to our rooms, I expected East to hand me a key, but he didn't. Instead he and Kaloni went into one room and Cali walked to the other. I followed Cali assuming we were sharing a room and inside I was smiling. I hoped we could make up because I needed to feel him inside of me. I was craving this nigga and bad. We walked in the room and I frowned at the double beds. This nigga was acting too damn petty for me. I stomped over to the bed that I was claiming and sat my suitcase down. I began unpacking my clothes, not saying shit to him. He did the same and that shit was starting to eat at me.

"If you gonna act like this, you could have just gotten me my own room."

"It ain't too late," he responded smartly.

"You know what, I'm tired of this shit. You trippin on me over a nigga I don't fuck with and never have. You mad because the nigga said I was leaving with him and you damn right I did. I mean come on, you were entertaining a bitch. And from what it looked like to me, you really like her!" I shouted and slammed my suitcase closed. "I don't fucking want him!" I stormed out the room and headed into the restroom.

I was so overwhelmed a few tears came down my face. I quickly wiped them because this wasn't me. I didn't get emotionally attached to niggas. Stripping out my clothing, I got into the shower. I let the hot water soothe me by letting it fall completely over my body even wetting my hair. I had my eyes closed and thoughts of the day Cali and I had sex during the party took over me. I just knew from that day we would be okay, but I guess not. I expected to lay with him and pour my heart out. I wanted to tell him about my upbringing and even confess to him what I did for a living. Whether he judged me or not, I wanted to open up to him and not hide anything from my man.

I opened my eyes to the sound of Cali's voice.

"Regardless of what I did, you shouldn't have never told the nigga you was going with him. That's hoe shit, Dreu, and the shit wasn't cool. That nigga said that shit in front of my peoples like I'm some sucka ass nigga. Had it not been for all those people, that nigga was gone be dead and his blood was gone be on your hands."

"I'm sorry," was all I could say.

I was done arguing. I was done beefing. I needed Cali in my good graces because I was losing it without him. I watched how Kaloni and East loved each other and I wanted that same love.

"Dreu, a nigga not playing with you. You keep testing me I'mma show you why they call me Calhoun," he said, seriously.

I guess that was his way of saying he forgave me because he began undressing. I swear you could hear my heartbeat through my chest. I had been dreading this moment for days.

When he climbed in, I stepped to the side so the water could relax him as it had done me. I watched Cali as the water dripped from his body and lord this was a sight to see. This man was perfect. His rock hard chest was covered in many tattoos all the way down to his arms. His dick was past hard nearly touching me where I stood.

Tonight, I was gonna do the unthinkable. I grabbed his tool and began slowly jacking it off. When he tilted his head back, I dropped to my knees and took him fully into my mouth with no effort. As I sucked him slowly, I looked up and he wore this look as if he couldn't believe I was doing this. He grabbed my head and that shit had my pussy juices mixing with the water. I pushed him against the porcelain wall, so I could take charge and before I knew it, I had a rhythm going that had him moaning.

I went up and down using as much tongue as I could. I slowly pulled up, then went all the way down trying hard not to gag. As I bopped up and down, I used my hand to massage his nuts. This really made him go crazy. I did this for about fifteen minutes and before I knew it, I could feel his dick harden. Believe it or not, I had never sucked a mans dick, let alone swallow a man's cum, but today that would change. I let him drop every ounce down my throat as I continued to suck. He gripped my head for me to stop, but I didn't. I pushed his hand away and continued to suck it until every last drop came out. Once I was done, I stood up and looked at him. We had an intimate stair down for quite some time and with our eyes, we communicated.

"What you tryna do to me, Dreu?" he said like a shaken eight-year-old.

"Whatever you let me do, Anthony. I just wanna make you happy. I just want you to love me," I told him, sincerely.

I waited for his response but I didn't get one. Instead we climbed out the shower and headed to the bed. The way his dick had bricked back up, I knew what that meant. And looking in his eyes, told me he was gonna punish my pussy. Guess what, a bitch was ready.

Fourteen
Kaloni

Today was our last day in Mexico and I knew I would miss this place. East promised to bring me back and I couldn't wait. Everything about the setting was perfect and especially because I had East right by my side. This man was really heaven sent. It took some time for me to adjust to his lifestyle and I was coming around. One thing about him was, he put me first. He didn't put me in harm's way and when it came to his business, I was a priority. Right now, we walked the beach and laughed at Dreu and Cali. These two argued all damn day, but they were in love. I'm so glad they made up because I could tell my best friend was going crazy without him.

"You trust me?" Cali asked Dreu.

"No, nigga. I don't trust you in that damn water," Dreu replied, making me laugh.

I looked at East, but I could tell he was thinking hard. His mind was elsewhere and it really wasn't my business.

"Man, I'm not gon' let you drown."

"No, nigga." Dreu replied.

Cali grabbed her, and she was screaming for dear life. I was so busy laughing I didn't notice East had walked off. From where I stood, I could see him. He looked like he was in a heated conversation on the phone. As Dreu and Cali began to play fight, my mind drifted off to the possibility of East cheating on me. I mean it was days he'd leave me saying he'd have business to handle and I wouldn't trip. Sometimes, he would turn his phone off and say he fell asleep. I would always shake the thoughts off giving him the benefit of the doubt. But I had one question I'd been meaning to ask; why he never took me to his house? He was rolling in dough, so I know his shit was laid. We would always stay at my house or get a room, so when we got back, I was gonna ask him.

After walking the beach, East had finally joined me. We went out to eat then headed for our hotel room to pack. East was a little distant, which was odd. We had been doing good this whole time. I wanted so bad to pry, but I was the type of person to mind my business. I couldn't help it though, shit was eating at me. I don't know if it was something I had done, but curiosity was getting the best of me.

"Bae, you good?" I asked him, looking up from my suitcase.

He looked at me and I could tell he was trying to choose his words wisely.

"I'm good ma," was all he said.

"No, you're not. I know you and you're not okay."

"I'm fine, Loni. Just shit on my mind about that business deal today."

I knew that was bullshit by the way he said it. What I also knew was, if anything was wrong, Cali would be spazzing out. I've been around these niggas long enough to know them.

"Can I go to your house when we get back?" I asked him, catching him off guard.

"Where that come from?" he asked with his face frowned up.

"I don't know, I was just thinking I've never been to your house. I mean we always stay at rooms or either at my house."

"Oh," was all he said.

I left the subject alone and finished packing. I had a gut feeling that something was really wrong with this picture, but like always, I left the shit alone.

~

"I just think you should investigate best. The nigga hiding something, don't be so gullible."

"It's not that I'm gullible, I just believe in people's privacy."

"Man fuck all that." Dreu waved her hand in the air. "You rather know than not know. Trust me, if the nigga playing you, I suggest you find out now before yo ass all crazy in love like that girl in the *Me U Hennessy* book."

"Her name was Raine and trust me that would never happen," I laughed because this girl was too damn dramatic.

"I'm telling you yo ass gone end up like her."

"I got a confession," I looked at her nervously.

"Yo' ass bet not be pregnant." She mugged me hard.

"Noooo silly." I fell out laughing. "On the way home, I snuck a picture of the registration to his car." I closed my eyes embarrassed.

I was waiting on Dreu to reply, but she never did, so I opened my eyes.

"Bitch, so what the fuck we waiting on?" She jumped up and grabbed her purse. I couldn't stop laughing. "Shit we just gone roll by see what we see. If we see the nigga car, then we knock."

"And what if he has company?"

"Then bitch I guess we throwing a party," she said and laughed.

It sounded good and that's exactly what it was, easier said than done.

Lord I hope I don't regret what I'm about to do.

When we pulled up to the address that Dreu had put into her Waze app, I noticed East's car out front along with a few other exotic cars. If this was this nigga's house, he was living large. A slight rage of jealousy came over me because like I said, I'd never been here. We sat in the car for some time just watching the home. Dreu kept saying for us to knock, but I was unsure about that. After about thirty minutes of debating back and forth, suddenly the front door came open and out walked a lady.

"Wait, I know that chick from somewhere, but I don't know where," Dreu said, studying the lady hard. I couldn't front if I wanted to, she was beautiful.

Moments later, East walked out behind her and went and stood by the vehicle she had climbed in. When the nigga bent down and pecked her on the lips, my heart sank.

"I knew it! I fucking knew it!" Dreu slammed her fist into her hand.

I wanted to get out badly, but I decided not to. I waited for East to head back into the house and listening to Dreu, we ended up following the car.

After trailing the car to Crenshaw Blvd., she pulled into the Baldwin Hills Mall. As soon as she parked, I got out of the car and approached her vehicle. Dreu was right behind me already talking shit.

"I got this, Dreu," I told her, so she could chill.

"Excuse me," I said as she got out of her car.

She looked at me curiously then to Dreu. It was something about the way she looked at Dreu that had me confused. She studied her as if she knew her from somewhere, but she quickly turned to look at me.

"Who are you? And what do you want with me?"

"I'm Kaloni. I just wanted to know umm...ummm."

"Who are you to East?" Dreu blurted out.

See Dreu was very confrontational. Her ass didn't have no filter.

"Let me guess you're one of his many flings," she said, raising her eyebrow.

"I'm not a fling I'm his girlfriend."

"Ha ha ha girl, is that what he tells you? Well, let me tell you this, I'm Jennifer his fiancé," she said, waving a huge diamond ring in my face. "We've been together for years and I ain't going anywhere," she said and stepped into my face. "Now, you and your little ghetto ass friend could run along because I ain't got the time."

"Ghetto? Oh, bitch I got your ghetto," Dreu said, taking off her earrings.

"I got this, Dreu." I put my hand up to let her know to chill.

"Well, fiancé, I guess he's both our man. And if you don't believe it, call him."

"Oh, baby you ain't said shit but a word." She pulled her phone from her hand bag and dialed East's number. Seconds later, he came through the phone all jittery and shit and that shit pissed me off more.

"Sup, baby you miss me already?"

"Well, I have someone here that misses you," she said, then turned the phone to me. The look on East's face was priceless.

"Loni," he mouthed my name, but in a low voice.

"Hey baby. You miss me, too, I hope," I smirked trying hard not to cry.

"Man, what type of games y'all playing?"

"We ain't playing shit. You a foul ass nigga. So, this the reason you never took me to your house huh?" I asked and the second I did, the call dropped, or the nigga hung up.

"Now is there anything else you need, because I have shopping to do," she said in a feisty demeanor.

Before I knew it, I hauled off and punched her in the mouth.

"That's right get that bitch bestie." Dreu was shouting from the sideline.

The more I heard her voice, the more pumped up I became. I began swinging like a wild bull. She was swinging, too, but her hits were not connecting. We fought for some time because I began to get tired. Before I knew it, the police had swooped up and pulled me off of her. Without warning, they threw me into the squad car and placed Jennifer in another car. She was screaming at the top of her lungs as I sat there now feeling dumb. I was about to go to jail over a nigga that wasn't even mine.

"I'm finna come get you," Dreu yelled out and headed to my car.

I knew she meant what she said about getting me out, but that wasn't the case. Tears began to fall from my eyes and I felt straight played. All along, this nigga was playing house while promising me the world. I'd never in my life felt so humiliated.

"Ma'am step out of the car." An officer opened my door for me to get out. When I climbed out, he pinned me against the car and began reading me my rights. What shocked the hell out of me was the part when he said, "You're under arrest for assault and battery on a pregnant woman." Again, my heart sank. When I saw Jennifer walking to her car scot-free, tears filled my eyes again. I couldn't believe what the fuck was going on.

Sigh.

～

When I got down to the precinct, I was quickly booked in and taken to the phone to make my one and only call. The only number I knew by heart was my mothers and Dreu's. I dialed Dreu's number and I could hear her arguing in the background. I knew more than likely it was Cali and now I cursed myself for not just calling my mother.

"Hey," I said into the phone sadly.

"You good?"

"Not really. They got me in here for battery and assault on a pregnant woman."

"What?!" she yelled out. "So, the bitch is pregnant?"

"Man, stay out they fucking business," I heard Cali say in the background.

"Nigga, fuck his business. This my fucking friend."

"So, how much is your bail?"

"It's 10 grand. If you can go to my mom's house and look in my pink box in the closet, there's money there from East. Fuck him, I'm using that shit."

"On god. Okay, I'm heading over there now."

"Okay, thank you," I told her and disconnected the line. I headed back to the holding tank and prayed they would hurry up before I was transferred.

Three hours later, I was walking out the cell a free woman. Although I was happy to be out, my heart ached like it had been ripped out my body and fed to lions. I had never in my life felt like this. If this is what love felt like, then I didn't want any parts of it. Now, I understood what Dreu meant and how she had a wall up as high as the Mexico wall Trump was trying to build. All I could think about was her warnings about messing with a *Dope Boy* and I should have listened.

When I stepped into the lobby, East sat in a chair with his head down. Instead of hurt, I became angry all over again. When he looked up, guilt was written all over his face. Right now, I didn't have shit to say to him. I was disgusted with just him being here.

"What you doing here?" I asked with my face frowned up.

"I had to come get you. The money you told Dreu to get wasn't right there."

"What you mean it wasn't there?"

"It wasn't there, Loni," he said and stood to his feet.

We walked out of the jail and headed towards my home. I was anxious to get home because I needed to make sure the money was there. Thoughts of my mother stealing from me crossed my mind. However, I knew my mother wouldn't do such a thing.

When we pulled up, I jumped out of East's car and ran full speed into my room. I went straight to the pink box I had stashed in my closet and the money was gone like he said. I then went and flipped over my mattress and nothing. I began rummaging through my drawers and I got the same results. I sat down on my bed and reality had began to sink in.

My mother had stolen my money. Right now, I had mixed emotions. I was furious and hurt at the same time. All these years of my life, my mother had never stolen from me. I was trying hard to justify for her, but who else could it have been? I know Dreu would never steal from me and no one had access to my room, but my mother. For the tenth time today, tears began to roll down my face. Just thinking about the shitty luck I was having, I was so lost. I sat on my bed and cried my eyes out for what seemed like forever.

The sound of my creaking door told me someone had come in. When I looked up, it was East. I dropped my head in shame because his money was gone. I don't know how, but I was determined to get him his money. He took a seat beside me, but didn't say a word. We both sat in silence and this what we both needed.

FOURTEEN

Kaloni

---

*T*oday was our last day in Mexico and I knew I would miss this place. East promised to bring me back and I couldn't wait. Everything about the setting was perfect and especially because I had East right by my side. This man was really heaven sent. It took some time for me to adjust to his lifestyle and I was coming around. One thing about him was, he put me first. He didn't put me in harm's way and when it came to his business, I was a priority. Right now, we walked the beach and laughed at Dreu and Cali. These two argued all damn day, but they were in love. I'm so glad they made up because I could tell my best friend was going crazy without him.

"You trust me?" Cali asked Dreu.

"No, nigga. I don't trust you in that damn water," Dreu replied, making me laugh.

I looked at East, but I could tell he was thinking hard. His mind was elsewhere and it really wasn't my business.

"Man, I'm not gon' let you drown."

"No, nigga." Dreu replied.

Cali grabbed her, and she was screaming for dear life. I was so busy laughing I didn't notice East had walked off. From where I stood, I could see him. He looked like he was in a heated conversation on the phone. As Dreu and Cali began to play fight, my mind drifted off to the possibility of East cheating on me. I mean it was days he'd leave me saying he'd have business to handle and I wouldn't trip. Sometimes, he would turn his phone off and say he fell asleep. I would always shake the thoughts off giving him the benefit of the doubt. But I had one question I'd been meaning to ask; why he never took me to his house? He was rolling in dough, so I know his shit was laid. We would always stay at my house or get a room, so when we got back, I was gonna ask him.

After walking the beach, East had finally joined me. We went out to eat then headed for our hotel room to pack. East was a little distant, which was odd. We had been doing good this whole time. I wanted so bad to pry, but I was the type of person to mind my business. I couldn't help it though, shit was eating at me. I don't know if it was something I had done, but curiosity was getting the best of me.

"Bae, you good?" I asked him, looking up from my suitcase.

He looked at me and I could tell he was trying to choose his words wisely.

"I'm good ma," was all he said.

"No, you're not. I know you and you're not okay."

"I'm fine, Loni. Just shit on my mind about that business deal today."

I knew that was bullshit by the way he said it. What I also knew was, if anything was wrong, Cali would be spazzing out. I've been around these niggas long enough to know them.

"Can I go to your house when we get back?" I asked him, catching him off guard.

"Where that come from?" he asked with his face frowned up.

"I don't know, I was just thinking I've never been to your house. I mean we always stay at rooms or either at my house."

"Oh," was all he said.

I left the subject alone and finished packing. I had a gut feeling that something was really wrong with this picture, but like always, I left the shit alone.

~

"I just think you should investigate best. The nigga hiding something, don't be so gullible."

"It's not that I'm gullible, I just believe in people's privacy."

"Man fuck all that." Dreu waved her hand in the air. "You rather know than not know. Trust me, if the nigga playing you, I suggest you find out now before yo ass all crazy in love like that girl in the *Me U Hennessy* book."

"Her name was Raine and trust me that would never happen," I laughed because this girl was too damn dramatic.

"I'm telling you yo ass gone end up like her."

"I got a confession," I looked at her nervously.

"Yo' ass bet not be pregnant." She mugged me hard.

"Noooo silly." I fell out laughing. "On the way home, I snuck a picture of the registration to his car." I closed my eyes embarrassed.

I was waiting on Dreu to reply, but she never did, so I opened my eyes.

"Bitch, so what the fuck we waiting on?" She jumped up and grabbed her purse. I couldn't stop laughing. "Shit we just gone roll by see what we see. If we see the nigga car, then we knock."

"And what if he has company?"

"Then bitch I guess we throwing a party," she said and laughed.

It sounded good and that's exactly what it was, easier said than done.

Lord I hope I don't regret what I'm about to do.

When we pulled up to the address that Dreu had put into her Waze app, I noticed East's car out front along with a few other exotic cars. If this was this nigga's house, he was living large. A slight rage of jealousy came over me because like I said, I'd never been here. We sat in the car for some time just watching the home. Dreu kept saying for us to knock, but I was unsure about that. After about thirty minutes of debating back and forth, suddenly the front door came open and out walked a lady.

"Wait, I know that chick from somewhere, but I don't know where," Dreu said, studying the lady hard. I couldn't front if I wanted to, she was beautiful.

Moments later, East walked out behind her and went and stood by the vehicle she had climbed in. When the nigga bent down and pecked her on the lips, my heart sank.

"I knew it! I fucking knew it!" Dreu slammed her fist into her hand.

I wanted to get out badly, but I decided not to. I waited for East to head back into the house and listening to Dreu, we ended up following the car.

After trailing the car to Crenshaw Blvd., she pulled into the Baldwin Hills Mall. As soon as she parked, I got out of the car and approached her vehicle. Dreu was right behind me already talking shit.

"I got this, Dreu," I told her, so she could chill.

"Excuse me," I said as she got out of her car.

She looked at me curiously then to Dreu. It was something about the way she looked at Dreu that had me confused. She studied her as if she knew her from somewhere, but she quickly turned to look at me.

"Who are you? And what do you want with me?"

"I'm Kaloni. I just wanted to know umm...ummm."

"Who are you to East?" Dreu blurted out.

See Dreu was very confrontational. Her ass didn't have no filter.

"Let me guess you're one of his many flings," she said, raising her eyebrow.

"I'm not a fling I'm his girlfriend."

"Ha ha ha girl, is that what he tells you? Well, let me tell you this, I'm Jennifer his fiancé," she said, waving a huge diamond ring in my face. "We've been together for years and I ain't going anywhere," she said and stepped into my face. "Now, you and your little ghetto ass friend could run along because I ain't got the time."

"Ghetto? Oh, bitch I got your ghetto," Dreu said, taking off her earrings.

"I got this, Dreu." I put my hand up to let her know to chill.

"Well, fiancé, I guess he's both our man. And if you don't believe it, call him."

"Oh, baby you ain't said shit but a word." She pulled her phone from her hand bag and dialed East's number. Seconds later, he came through the phone all jittery and shit and that shit pissed me off more.

"Sup, baby you miss me already?"

"Well, I have someone here that misses you," she said, then turned the phone to me. The look on East's face was priceless.

"Loni," he mouthed my name, but in a low voice.

"Hey baby. You miss me, too, I hope," I smirked trying hard not to cry.

"Man, what type of games y'all playing?"

"We ain't playing shit. You a foul ass nigga. So, this the reason you never took me to your house huh?" I asked and the second I did, the call dropped, or the nigga hung up.

"Now is there anything else you need, because I have shopping to do," she said in a feisty demeanor.

Before I knew it, I hauled off and punched her in the mouth.

"That's right get that bitch bestie." Dreu was shouting from the sideline.

The more I heard her voice, the more pumped up I became. I began swinging like a wild bull. She was swinging, too, but her hits were not connecting. We fought for some time because I began to get tired. Before I knew it, the police had swooped up and pulled me off of her. Without warning, they threw me into the squad car and placed Jennifer in another car. She was screaming at the top of her lungs as I sat there now feeling dumb. I was about to go to jail over a nigga that wasn't even mine.

"I'm finna come get you," Dreu yelled out and headed to my car.

I knew she meant what she said about getting me out, but that wasn't the case. Tears began to fall from my eyes and I felt straight played. All along, this nigga was playing house while promising me the world. I'd never in my life felt so humiliated.

"Ma'am step out of the car." An officer opened my door for me to get out. When I climbed out, he pinned me against the car and began reading me my rights. What shocked the hell out of me was the part when he said, "You're under arrest for assault and battery on a pregnant woman." Again, my heart sank. When I saw Jennifer walking to her car scot-free, tears filled my eyes again. I couldn't believe what the fuck was going on.

Sigh.

When I got down to the precinct, I was quickly booked in and taken to the phone to make my one and only call. The only number I knew by heart was my mothers and Dreu's. I dialed Dreu's number and I could hear her arguing in the background. I knew more than likely it was Cali and now I cursed myself for not just calling my mother.

"Hey," I said into the phone sadly.

"You good?"

"Not really. They got me in here for battery and assault on a pregnant woman."

"What?!" she yelled out. "So, the bitch is pregnant?"

"Man, stay out they fucking business," I heard Cali say in the background.

"Nigga, fuck his business. This my fucking friend."

"So, how much is your bail?"

"It's 10 grand. If you can go to my mom's house and look in my pink box in the closet, there's money there from East. Fuck him, I'm using that shit."

"On god. Okay, I'm heading over there now."

"Okay, thank you," I told her and disconnected the line. I headed back to the holding tank and prayed they would hurry up before I was transferred.

Three hours later, I was walking out the cell a free woman. Although I was happy to be out, my heart ached like it had been ripped out my body and fed to lions. I had never in my life felt like this. If this is what love felt like, then I didn't want any parts of it. Now, I understood what Dreu meant and how she had a wall up as high as the Mexico wall Trump was trying to build. All I could think about was her warnings about messing with a *Dope Boy* and I should have listened.

When I stepped into the lobby, East sat in a chair with his head down. Instead of hurt, I became angry all over again. When he looked up, guilt was written all over his face. Right now, I didn't have shit to say to him. I was disgusted with just him being here.

"What you doing here?" I asked with my face frowned up.

"I had to come get you. The money you told Dreu to get wasn't right there."

"What you mean it wasn't there?"

"It wasn't there, Loni," he said and stood to his feet.

We walked out of the jail and headed towards my home. I was anxious to get home because I needed to make sure the money was there. Thoughts of my mother stealing from me crossed my mind. However, I knew my mother wouldn't do such a thing.

When we pulled up, I jumped out of East's car and ran full speed into my room. I went straight to the pink box I had stashed in my closet and the money was gone like he said. I then went and flipped over my mattress and nothing. I began rummaging through my drawers and I got the same results. I sat down on my bed and reality had began to sink in.

My mother had stolen my money. Right now, I had mixed emotions. I was furious and hurt at the same time. All these years of my life, my mother had never stolen from me. I was trying hard to justify for her, but who else could it have been? I know Dreu would never steal from me and no one had access to my room, but my mother. For the tenth time today, tears began to roll down my face. Just thinking about the shitty luck I was having, I was so lost. I sat on my bed and cried my eyes out for what seemed like forever.

The sound of my creaking door told me someone had come in. When I looked up, it was East. I dropped my head in shame because his money was gone. I don't know how, but I was determined to get him his money. He took a seat beside me, but didn't say a word. We both sat in silence and this what we both needed.

FIFTEEN

East
─────────

*O*ther than my love life, shit was going pretty good. Just as Drak had promised, he upped our shipment by a hundred birds. This was all the fuck we needed because now we would be tripling our pay. Cali said this would be a bad move, but right now, I couldn't tell. His bitch ass was smiling from ear to ear as the workers unloaded the truck. Moving each brick one by one, I did a mind count. We copped each brick for $11,000 and we would sell them at twenty-one a piece. Which meant we would be profiting $3,000,000 in one shipment, which was music to my mind.

I walked into the warehouse into the room we cooked in. Cali was standing over the stove looking like a mad scientist. He had on a lab coat that he left open with his damn chain on. The nigga wore face goggles and a pair of gloves. I immediately fell out laughing.

"Fuck you laughing at?" he looked from the Pyrex jar.

This nigga had all four ranges going at one time with boiling water on each. I couldn't front this nigga was a good as cook. And the way he was maneuvering between all fires, had me impressed.

"Yo dumb ass looking like Einstein."

"Fuck you nigga. I am Einstein."

"Yeah, and tell me this was not a good move?"

"It's good money. But my nigga is it a good move?" he said and stepped closer to me. "You been watching too many movies and reading to many *Barbie Scott* books. We don't have the police in our pockets. The more money, the more heat from the law. Yo ass just better be ready."

He turned from me and pulled his goggles down.

I understood what he meant, but a nigga needed money. I wasn't content with what I had and especially because what I was about to do. I was gonna cop Kaloni a house and get her back in my good graces. After her mom stole that bread, she felt she was in debt to me, but little did she know, she only owed me her heart.

Since Kaloni wasn't fucking with me right now, I used this as my time to get Jenn back on my good side. After pleading and begging, I finally got her to talk to me. I wined and dined her, then put the *D* down on her and we were back. I told her I never smashed Kaloni and she believed it. However, she knew I liked her, because of the way I acted on the phone the day they fought. I made all these bull-shit promises that I knew I wouldn't be able to hold up on, but I would try. My next mission was to get Kaloni back. She hadn't spoken to me in weeks and I let her have her space. I had too much shit going on with this shipment and this shit was important.

Jacob: *I got that info bro*

I looked down at the text from my little brother. After reading it, I looked over at Cali and contemplated if I wanted to tell him. I knew he was gonna be happy to hear this shit because he wanted that nigga Brick's head. The nigga constantly talked about wanting to up the product because of the police, but shit killing was gonna alert them too. This nigga could be backwards sometimes and it wasn't shit I could do. If Cali said he wanted a nigga dead, then trust me, he was gonna die. Deciding I would handle this shit myself, I left him over the stove. I hit Jacob back and told him I'd be by tomorrow.

After Cali and I were done cooking up some work, we headed into the rest of the warehouse to instruct the ladies on what needed to be done. I took my seat in the back and let Cali take the center of the stage.

"Shit about to get real real, so if y'all can't handle it, I advise you to get the fuck out my establishment," he said and looked around to all the ladies. "We got more product, which means more work. I'mma bring in a few more women to help y'all ,but that don't mean for y'all to slack. Now, if you got shit to do in your daily living, please let me know a couple days in advance, so I could bring in a filler. I'mma gonna double everyone's pay starting tonight." When he said that, the ladies began to cheer him on. The cocky ass nigga started laughing. "I'mma give y'all a break tonight, so everyone take the day off." The ladies really began to cheer. "I need y'all here at 6:00 am sharp." It's like he didn't have to tell them again. They all walked off towards the rooms we had lockers built in for their clothing. Well, everybody but Lonyell. She stayed back to talk to Cali, so I walked off to make a quick call.

Dialing Kaloni's number, I knew she wouldn't answer, but I tried anyway. Hearing her sweet voice over the voicemail, I hung up and dialed her number again. To my surprise, she answered so a nigga was smiling.

"What Elijah?" she said, sarcastically.

"I need to see you."

"For what?"

"Because I got something for you."

"I don't need nothing from you and soon as I can, I'mma pay you back the money my mom stole."

"Man, I told you it's cool. Have you seen her, though?"

"No, she hasn't been home since." She sounded like she was

ready to cry. Despite her mother being on drugs, she loved that lady to death, so I knew this was weighing heavily on her.

"We need to find her ma. I'mma holla at a few of my peoples too, aight?"

"Okay," she responded, changing her tone.

I knew she was beginning to worry because her mother had just vanished. In Kaloni's mind her mother was in some sort of trouble, but me knowing how smokers got down, she was somewhere having a crack party.

"I'mma see you in a minute." I hung up before she could object.

When I walked back into the room to tell Cali I was bouncing, I couldn't do shit but laugh. Lonyell was down on her knees sucking the life out his dick. He looked over at me.

"You want some?" he said, holding her head with one hand.

"Nah, nigga I'm straight." I chuckled and went to head out the door. I stopped in my tracks when I heard voices in the front. I could hear a chick arguing with Big Russ and that voice belonged to nobody but Dreu.

"Nigga, Dreu out there," I told him, and he hurried to shove his dick back into his pants. He rushed out the room leaving Lonyell on her knees. I shook my head, laughing because she looked mad as hell. "This nigga, Cali wild," I said closing the door.

When I walked into the room where Cali and Dreu were, she looked me up and down.

"What's up, Dreu?"

"What's up with skinless ass?" she said, smirking.

"Man stall my nigga out."

"Nope he foul."

"Y'all nosey asses ain't even have no business going to that man's house," Cali said in my defense.

"And he had no business playing my friend."

"Man, mind yo business," Cali said, grilling her.

"See you tomorrow, Cali." We all turned around to the voice of Lonyell.

She was fully dressed and had her duffle bag thrown over her shoulder. She was smiling hard, which let me know she was doing the shit on purpose. Cali didn't do shit but nod his head because his ass was too damn guilty. Had Dreu not been here and she pulled that shit, Cali would be going smooth upside her head.

"You fucking this bitch?" Dreu asked, snapping her neck.

"Nah, man you trippin," Cali said. I couldn't help it, I began to laugh hard. I never in my entire life seen someone have any type of mind control over this nigga.

"I ain't trippin shit. I swear I find out you fucking her, I'mma fuck you and that bitch up," Dreu said and shoved him in the head.

"Dreu, get that fucking finger out my face before I shoot the muthafucka off yo," Cali told her and that nigga was serious as fuck. I shook my head.

I headed out the door and climbed into my whip. I contemplated my next move. My mind was saying go home to Jenn, but my heart was saying run to Kaloni. Following my heart and dick, I drove out to Kaloni's crib full speed. I needed to see my baby like now.

On my way to Kaloni's, I stopped by one our traps to drop off the work Jock called for. Walking in, I dropped the duffle bag on the front table and went into the room to holler at a worker who worked for Jock named Kareem.

"How shit been going round here?" I asked Kareem who sat in front of a triple beam scale.

"Sup Boss. Shit been pretty cool. We moving this shit like a muthafucka. Who cooked it?"

"Fuck you mean who cooked it?"

"Cali," we both said at the same time and laughed.

"Yeah, that nigga whipped it," I admitted. "Fuck you trying to say, though?" I playfully punched him.

Kareem was my little nigga. He was a young ass savage. Nigga was only nineteen and I liked the way he moved. I was ready to cut Jock off and make him lieutenant of this trap because Jock was moving too weird these days. He was still in his feelings about us firing Pete because they were cousins. The nigga needed to understand Cali's logic. We didn't need no weak links on our team. He begged for us to give the nigga his job back, but Cali wasn't trying to hear that shit.

"Where Jock at?"

"Nigga said he had some shit to do." I shook my head. This nigga was acting like we were running a fucking cleaning service or some shit.

"Aight I'mma holla at that nigga."

"Fasho."

"You straight in here, though?"

"Yeah I'm good bro. Once the sun goes down, I'mma serve out the slot. And I got Patty & Gladys with me.

"Who the fuck is Patti and Gladys?" I asked confused.

When he lifted up his two chrome nines, I fell out laughing. This young nigga was wild, but I had to give it to him he had heart.

"Aight nigga. Well stay up and if you need me, I'll be around the corner."

"Aight." We slapped hands and I made my way out the door.

Hopping into my whip, I sent Kaloni a text to open the front door. Before I pulled off, I noticed Jock hopping out a black Lexus with dark ass tents. I sat back and watched his demeanor and he looked like he was up to something. The car pulled off fast and he quickly ran into the house. I brushed it off and pulled off to Kaloni's. Whatever this nigga was up to, he would soon reveal himself.

SIXTEEN

Calhoun

---

*C*ruising down Western Ave in my candy red 6 foe, I looked over at Dreu as her hair blew in the wind. We had the top back enjoying the weather. We were on our way to cruise with the cars on Manchester, then we were going to hit the beach house. Tonight, I had something special for Dreu. I was gonna show her a hood nigga could be romantic. I had this chick named Takiya from a company called *Picnics of Purpose* set us up a nice candle light dinner by the water. Right now, I was trying to kill time to make sure everything was perfect.

When we pulled into the Shell Gas Station, it was packed as usual. Cars were doing donuts in the middle of the streets and everyone pretty much chilled. There were all types of whips from monster trucks to SS's and plenty lowriders. Dreu looked on as the cars swerved through the streets. To her, this wasn't shit. When you lived in Cali, Sunday funday was a normal.

When I hopped out my whip, everyone was saying my name like a chant. Niggas I didn't know spoke, but I kept it moving. I damn near knew the whole city, but I wasn't a friendly nigga. Seeing some familiar faces, I made my way to my boy Whip who was with my other nigga Bugsy. It was crazy because Whip was a blood and

Bugsy was a crip, but they were brothers. These were the coolest niggas on this side of town and anytime I came to the West Side, I fucked with them. Whip had the coldest Malibu wagon with a fire concept paint and Bugsy had a Tan and Red SS Monte Carlo that had a cold ass motor.

"Hey Calhoun," some chick said, walking by with a group of her friends.

She was bad as fuck, but she wasn't fucking with Dreu. She tried to throw a little sass in her walk and hell yeah me, Bugsy, and Whip was watching.

I looked towards the car at Dreu, but she was busy enjoying the show. Before I knew it, her ass hopped out the car looking around for me. When she spotted me, she headed in my direction. It seemed like every nigga out here broke they neck watching her.

"Damn my nigga, they on yo bitch," Whip said laughing.

"Niggas get they head knocked off," I told him, seriously.

"What's up ma?"

"I need something to drink," she said and walked into the gas station.

Three chicks walked over to us and started talking to Bugsy. When my phone alerted me, I had a text, I knew it was prolly Takiya, which meant everything was ready. I dapped Bugsy and Whip up then headed to the car to wait for Dreu.

When we pulled up to the crib, I told Dreu to go change into the dress I had copped her that was laying on my bed. I made sure to tell her not to wear any panties and she smirked. I went into the kitchen and grabbed two bottles of Ace I had in the fridge. I walked outside to wait for Dreu and I made sure to leave the door open to give her a hint to follow. When I walked over to the table, a nigga was taken aback at how nice the set up was.

Music played, there was an elegant tablecloth on the table that was adorned with rose petals. In the middle of the table, held two tall candles with red bow ties. I don't know why, but I felt kind of nervous because a nigga ain't never did no shit like this. I took a seat and popped open a bottle. I began looking out into the ocean and the shit took my mind to a whole other place. I tried not to think of the streets, but it was hard. My main focus was always on money, so I was trying to shake the thoughts and finally relax.

"Awe Baby!" I heard her voice behind me. I turned to look at her and she was smiling from ear to ear. "So, you do have a romantic side?" she smirked before taking a seat. I pulled the glass from the cooler and began pouring her a drink.

I got a lil' hoe at V-Live
   She got her butt tatted on each side
   I like her, she a boss and she don't D ride
   And I wear the pants, she don't decide
   Don't talk about your ex, you know he mad
   Bad bitch, you conceited

Lil Durk "Homebody" played in the background. I wasn't no love music type nigga so this is what I selected.

"I wanted to do something nice for my baby."

"This is nice," she said and reached over to kiss me.

"Dreu, you love me?" I asked her, because I needed to be sure. I had plans for baby girl and I wanted to make sure I didn't make a mistake.

"Of course, I love you, Anthony," she said, looking nervous. I knew she loved me just by the way she said my name. I nodded my head and raised my glass.

"Ohh, what's this?" she said, lifting the iron trays that contained the steak, lobster, calamari and garlic spinach. "Ohh, I'm bout to fuck this up." She danced in her seat.

"Fat ass," I laughed.

"You love my fat ass," she said then looked at me for my response.

I really didn't know what to say because I had never actually told her I loved her. Instead of responding, I looked off into the water.

"It's okay to be in love, Cali," she said, shocking the hell out of me.

"Is that right Ms. I don't love these niggas Miller."

"All that has changed thanks to you. Trust me if I can let my guards down and love, I need you to meet me halfway," she said and picked up my lobster. I thought about what she said as I watched her. She broke my lobster in half and pulled it from the shell. She then did the same thing to hers.

"Do you miss your family?" she asked me, changing the subject.

"I miss the thought of having a family. I was too young to remember anything about them." I responded, nonchalantly.

"You miss yours?"

"Well, I had been raised by my grandma, so she's all that matter to me. But yeah, I miss my mom. Although he did what she did, I can't take away the fact that she was a great mother. I was young when she passed, but I have a lot of great memories."

"When you gone let me meet my g moms?" I smirked at her.

"You ready for that?" You know when you meet her that means we getting married," she smirked, batting her eyes.

"Let's go get in the water," I told her as I wiped my mouth. She looked out into the water and I could see she was hesitant.

"Come on ma, you trust me, don't you?" I asked her this question a million times and for the first time, she nodded her head yes.

I grabbed her hand and helped her stand to her feet. I wrapped my arms around her and began to kiss her neck. She then turned around to me and looked me in the eyes.

"I love you, Cali," she said with so much sincerity that I had no choice but to say it back.

"I love you too ma." I pulled her close to me and kissed her again.

Normally, Dreu would either hold back or she would kiss me like we were fucking. Right now, something felt different about the kiss. It was passionate.

"Cali, please don't hurt me," she whispered out into the air, but loud enough for me to hear her. Promise me you won't hurt me."

"I prom..."

"Oh, isn't this cute." I was cut off by Jazz's voice.

When I turned around, she was standing there with her arms folded and I could see the hurt all over her face. *Damn;* I thought to myself as I looked from her to Dreu who was now staring at me ready for some shit to pop off. I shook my head and thought about what I was gonna say. *Reverse psychology.*

"Why the fuck you popping up to my crib?"

"Maybe if you answer your fucking phone sometimes, I wouldn't have to just pop up. So, this what it is, Cali? I mean, from what I see you, you feeling this chick. You ain't never did no shit like this for me," she began rambling. "Girl you lucky," she said looking at Dreu. Dreu stood there motionless and I knew what that shit meant. She was waiting for Jazz to say the wrong shit, so she could go crazy.

"Jazz, just get the fuck on."

"Oh, that's what you really want? Because you know if I leave, I'm never coming back."

"And you saying that like I need you. Remember who the fuck I am shorty. I don't need no bitch!" The sound of my voice made her jump.

"So, is this your girl now?" she said on the verge of crying. But by this time, I was mad as fuck.

"You damn right this my bitch. Look around my nigga, you think I would be doing all this for a jumpoff?" I had my arms open, so she could get the picture.

"So, that's all I was was a jumpoff?" she asked, now crying.

"Come here, Dreu." I called Dreu over to me.

When she walked over to me, I kissed her in the mouth hard. I knew this would get to Jazz because I never kissed her. I never really kissed no bitch, but Ayanna.

When I let Dreu go, she was smiling hard as she wiped my spit from around her lips.

"Now, I hope that's all the confirmation you needed," I told her then turned to walk away.

"Well, I hope you're happy," she said and walked off. Before she was out of ears reach, she turned around and said.

"I hope she's ready to play step mama." She nodded to Dreu then stormed off. Dreu looked at me and I know I was pale in the face.

"This bitch is pregnant?" Dreu said with her head cocked to the side.

I could see the hurt all in her face and before I could respond, tears began to pour from her eyes. When she stormed off, I kicked the table over that held the food and candles. I couldn't believe this shit was happening. The night was so perfect, and I had finally told this girl I loved her and here comes this bitch Jazz with this shit. It's like I couldn't win from losing.

SEVENTEEN

Dreu

I sat in my trap hustling my ass off trying to get my mind off Cali. It was like whenever I couldn't figure shit out, I would run to my trap. This was the only place I could unwind because it was always some excitement. If I were in my bedroom, I'd prolly just cry all damn day. Brick had just brought me some work, so I knew I would be here for about a week. I was gonna shut down on the world and even my best friend. I know she needed me, but she was fine. East was working his way back in, so I knew for a fact she was back to being happy and in love, which is why I was gonna shut down.

I was a broken-hearted bitch right now, so I didn't want to damper her mood. Not only that, but she was already going through enough. After her mother had stolen the money, she basically disappeared. Kaloni was starting to worry about her, but I knew better. Pearl was somewhere blowing that money on a crack high.

"What's wrong with you child?" Brenda asked, taking a seat next to me.

Because I never really got personal with Brenda, I was reluctant on telling her what was going on. Other than her cooking for me, we were business only. But because I didn't have anyone to talk to, I was gonna fill her in. I let out a deep sigh and she gave me a look as if she knew what was wrong.

"Who is he?" was all she said.

"His name is Calhoun, but everyone calls him Cali." I looked at her. The look on her face immediately dropped, so I assumed she knew who he was. It really didn't surprise me because the love Cali got in the streets told me he had a huge reputation. "You know him?" I asked her because she still had this look on her face I couldn't read.

"I've heard of him," was all she said. I mean Brenda was a drug user, so I was more than sure she heard his name being mentioned. "So, what's going on with you guys? I mean one minute you're happy and the next you looking like you lost your best friend.

"It feels like it." I looked out the huge picture window. I began explaining to her how I didn't want to be involved with anyone and up until the dinner he had set up on the beach. When I told her about Jazz popping, up her mouth dropped.

"Well, I think you should hear him out. She could be lying. And if she isn't, remember she was here before you came along. That man probably don't even want her baby."

"True, but I don't know, Brenda. I don't think I can deal with all the baby mama drama that's gonna come along with it.

"You're right because I went through it with Charles. Honey I fought, stabbed, stalked and everything above for that man. I eventually won him, but I was scared. The girl ended up being pregnant and she used that baby to make my life a living hell." She shook her head and looked out the window. Birds flew through the sky and we both were in a daze.

"Run on and get your clothes. I'mma gonna make you some Oxtails and rice," Brenda said, knocking me out my thoughts.

"Okay. I'll be right back," I said excited. Ms. Brenda knew how to cook, and I loved every dish she made. I went into my room and stashed my work then headed for the door.

Walking up the street, I noticed a Chevy Impala sitting out front of my granny's house. I was looking hard because I didn't recognize the car. When I got closer, I scrunched my face up because Kendall had hopped out the driver's seat.

Shit. I cursed myself because this nigga was a bugaboo. He walked over to the curb and stood directly in front of my home.

"I know you been seeing my calls?"

"What are you calling me for? I told you I'm cool."

"Man, you ain't never cool."

"It's been a year." I rolled my eyes upset. "What do you..." I said but was cut off by the sound of a dirt bike. I knew it couldn't be anybody but Cali so my heart began to beat faster.

"Kendall, you need to leave."

"I ain't leaving until you talk to me."

"I'm telling you now you need to go," I told him just as Cali pulled up in front of where we stood. He removed his helmet then climbed off his bike. He was mugging the shit out of me and then mugged Kendall.

"You don't see me calling you," he said with so much aggression.

"No, Cali, I don't. And bye, Kendall," I told the both of them. I didn't have shit to say to Kendall and right now, I wasn't ready to talk to Cali.

"Who the fuck is you?" Cali asked, walking up on Kendall.

"Her nigga. Who is you?" Kendall shot.

"I'm not your girl." I looked at Kendall and before I knew it, Cali and swung on him and knocked him out cold. He began stomping him out and I started screaming for dear life.

"Cali! Stop!" I cried out, but he wasn't trying to hear it. "Cali you're gonna kill him," I said and snatched him back. Just because I wasn't fucking with Kendall didn't mean I wanted to be a witness to his assault. Kendall was a really nice guy so seeing Cali destroy him had me feeling sorry for him.

"What the hell y'all got going on out here?" the sound of my granny's voice made Cali and I turn around. Kendall was still knocked out and bleeding badly.

"He got knocked the fuck out." My little brother laughed standing beside my granny.

"Boy get yo ass in the house." My granny said shoving him into the house.

"Get yo shit and let's roll," Cali said as he massaged his knuckles.

"I'm not leaving with you, Cali." I stormed into the house. I left him and Kendall right outside. I went into my room and grabbed my clothing, so I could go back to Brenda's.

As I was packing my clothing, Cali pushed my room door open. I ignored him and kept moving around my room. He walked up to me and snatched my bag from my hand. He slammed me down on the bed then went to lock my door. Seconds later, there was a knock at the door. I looked at him and went to unlock it. It was Micah.

"Boy, what you want?" he was standing there with a basketball in his hand.

"Man, you knocked that nigga out," he said excited.

"Boy, watch yo mouth." I lifted up from the bed.

"Stall little man out," Cali said with a hand gesture. "Come here little man. What's your name?"

"Micah."

"How old are you?"

"I'mma be twelve next month. My GG throwing me a party," he said smiling.

"Here little man. Buy you something for your birthday." Cali pulled out a wad of money and handed it to him.

"Micah! Get yo butt out of here." my granny said, walking to my door. "Boy you in here begging," she said noticing the money in Micah's hand.

"He's good, Mrs. Miller," Cali said shocking me. I didn't think he remembered my granny's name.

"Ohhh I got. 1, 2, 3, 4, 5 hundred dollars," Micah said counting his money. This boy had $500 dollars and was too happy.

"Where mine?" My granny said, smirking at Cali.

"You can have the world GG," he said and pulled his money back out. I tried hard to count the money he handed her, but it was too much. It had to be at least ten grand. She started smiling and waving the money around like she hit the jackpot.

"You can come and go as you please son. Just don't knock no more niggas out in my front lawn," she laughed and closed the door.

"Thanks, Cali, you just bought my damn family from me," I told him and rolled my eyes.

"Can I buy you, too?" he said and went into his pocket.

"I can't be bought," I said, getting emotional.

"I don't wanna buy you, Dreu. I want your love at no cost ma. Matter fact, fuck that, I need your love. I need you, Dreu," he said, looking me in my eyes. I'm not worried bout this bitch Jazz and on my life, I'mma do everything I can to make that bitch get an abortion." He took a seat on my bed.

"And what if she don't?"

"For you." he looked at me with bloodshot red eyes. "I'mma kill her," he said like it was nothing. Something deep down, told me he was serious. "Now what's up with this clown that you was outside talking to?"

"He's my ex."

"You been fucking with that nigga?"

"No."

"Don't test me, Dreu," he said and stood to his feet. "Now get yo shit let's roll." He walked out the door. I let out a deep sigh. This shit with Cali was complicating my life more and more by the days, but for some reason I was loving it. Now as far as that baby, I guess we'd cross that bridge when it came.

EIGHTEEN

East

───────────

"*W*here you going ma?" I asked Jennifer as she grabbed her bag. I really didn't care where she was going because I needed to get back to Kaloni. I promised her we were going to dinner and I wanted to keep my word.

"I'm going out with Regina."

"Where y'all going?"

"Out," she said and smiled.

"Aight, well I'mma run to the warehouse and check on that shit."

"Okay, well I'll see you later, right?" she asked.

"Yeah. I'll be home kinda late, though."

"Okay. Take your time, I know you got work to do." She kissed my cheek.

"Aight be safe."

I grabbed my keys and headed out the door right behind Jenny. When I got into my car, I watched her as she hopped on her phone. Just knowing I was running off to Kaloni, I felt bad. I knew sooner or later shit was gonna change because Jenny was now pregnant. The news to me was shocking and Kaloni is the one that told me. When I asked Jenny about it, she claimed she wanted to surprise me and trust me she did more than just that. I didn't have any kids and I wouldn't mind having one with Jenn. Then again, now I had Kaloni in my life I was confused. Kaloni was still kind of distant because of the situation and there wasn't shit I could say. Not only did I lie about having a girl, but she was now pregnant.

When Jenny pulled off, I pulled off heading in the opposite direction. I looked at my clock and I had a little time to kill before I went to get Kaloni, so I decided to just go holla at Jacob.

When I pulled to my mom's crib, I got out the whip reluctantly and headed to the door. I knocked twice, and my step pops opened the door.

"Hey son," he said closing the door behind us.

My step pops was cool as an A/C unit. It was my mom that wore the pants so this nigga didn't have a say so on how she treated me. As much as I despised my mom, I still sent money to my step pops account to make sure they were straight. For years, I held a grudge, but once life got good, I couldn't help it. This was my mama.

"East," was all she said not moved by my presence.

"Mom," I matched her tone and headed straight for Jacob's cave, as he called it. When I walked in, he was behind his computer like always.

"What you got for me little peanut head ass boy?" I said, taking a seat in his lazy boy chair.

"I got some good shit. I was even able to track his phone. I have it set up on another cellular I'm gonna give you, so you can track him. First and foremost, he supplies four trap houses and one close to you on 39th and Stanford."

When he said that my eyes popped out. That was the same spot Pete was watching for us and had got shot at. All he said was it was some bitch and he didn't know nothing else.

"Also, here's his name, address, his next to kin and anything else you need," he handed me a long as piece of paper.

As I read the paper I was shocked. I wasn't surprised by Jacobs finding because I knew he was sharp. I was more ecstatic because this nigga Brick was too close to home. I read all his addresses and when I say, too close to home, this nigga Mama lived in the hood. That alone let me know he wasn't shit. He was running traps, but his mama still lived in the trenches. That was rule number one to a D Boy; move yo mama away before you buy your own first house.

"Everything you got is right there. I'm bout to go get some pussy." He stood up smiling.

"Boy yo ass a virgin," I teased him.

"I got way more bitches than you. Bet," he said laughing.

"Bet nigga," I laughed with him.

I playfully punched him and stood to leave. I hugged my bro then went into my pocket and handed him some bread. His face lit up with a huge smile. I gave him five bands for his work and a little extra for his pockets.

As I passed my moms, we both locked eyes and her being the witch she is, she turned her nose up and focused on something that wasn't even interesting. I walked out and hopped in my car. I checked the phone Jacob had given me and began my investigation on this nigga Brick. Instead of going towards Kaloni's crib, I followed the map towards where Brick was. I was just gonna watch this nigga moves for a minute then come back to finish tomorrow. I wanted to know this nigga every move and before I killed him, I was gonna rob his ass.

"Ayo, nigga I got that info," I told Cali.

I wasn't gonna say shit, but I had to tell him this nigga Brick was the one behind the spot that was slowing down our bread.

"Tell me something good"

"That spot on Naomi, that be slowing our paypa down and we put Pete on."

"What about it?"

"That nigga Brick runs it."

"Is that right?"

"Hell yeah. I'm sitting outside the crib right now."

"You see him?"

"Nah. I'm just sitting in the car. But the plate number I got, the whip right here."

"Aight good, good. Get that nigga and bring him to me East."

"I'll try nigga."

"Man just snatch the nigga yo," he said sounding upset.

"I gotta go. The nigga coming out now," I told Cali then hung up on him.

I reached into my waistband and pulled out my glock. I made sure the safety was off then tucked it back in my pants. He climbed into his whip and pulled off. I trailed behind him, but I made sure to stay a few cars behind. I don't know where this nigga was going, but I didn't give a fuck if he was driving to Texas, I was gonna follow.

Kaloni began blowing me up, but I couldn't answer her. I let the phone ring until the voicemail came on. When she called back, I powered my phone off and tossed it in the glove box. I knew she was gonna be pissed and because I didn't involve her in my street business. I didn't know what explanation I was gonna use.

Thirty minutes later, Bricks car pulled into a small motel located off La Brea. I could tell it was a cheap motel that rented by the hour, but the muthafucka was hella cool. It was lowkey and every car parked out front was nice. I watched as a Hispanic couple went inside, but Brick never moved from his car. He hopped on his phone and placed a call. I wanted so bad to just run down on him and knock his dick in the dirt, but I chose to play shit cool. I was more than sure there was cameras everywhere and today I was driving a whip that was in my name. A gangsta yes, a fool no, I'd never shit where I laid. So, I was gonna have to catch this nigga on a rebound.

Moments later, he climbed out the car and the door came ajar. I noticed a female figure as he reached out to give her a hug. When I got a better look, my heart dropped. *Jennifer?* I asked myself as if this shit was an illusion. My blood pressure rose up and my first reaction was grab my strap. This bitch and this nigga was gonna die today.

NINETEEN

Calhoun

---

3 0 mins before....

"So, is that your girlfriend?"

"No."

"I couldn't tell, the way she was acting at the block party."

"That's just my friend." I don't know why I lied, but for some reason I couldn't keep it real with Ayanna. It's like she held a spot in my heart that wouldn't let me 86 her completely.

"It's getting late," she said and yawned. I took that as my cue to leave.

"Yeah, I'mma get out of here." I told her and stood up.

I was happy anyway because had I stayed here a second later, I would have seduced her. She was looking good as fuck in her white v neck tee and the boy shorts she was wearing was hugging her fat ass tight.

Ayanna and I had been texting each other since the day she text when I was out of town. Because Dreu and I had made up, I didn't get a chance to take her out like I promised. I lied and told her I was gone longer than expected. Since I'd been back, she had been hitting me up. Today when she hit me, I promised I'd drop by and I kept my word. I had been here for a couple hours just enjoying her company. I had dropped Dreu off this morning because she said she had something to do. I ain't gone lie, a nigga was missing her crazy ass. Sitting here with Ayanna was making me feel guilty as fuck, which was another reason I was happy we were departing.

Ayanna was fine as fuck; still, but I wasn't trying to step out on Dreu. I had promised baby girl I wouldn't hurt her, and I was trying to keep my word. A nigga had done so much foul shit to her in so little time, I didn't want to put her through anything else.

"I'll see you soon?" Ayanna said, but more of a question.

"Yeah, ma. I'll see you soon." She hit me with a huge smile that light up the entire living room.

"Bye Anthony," again she smiled.

"Bye Yanni bear."

"Oh, my God I haven't heard that in years," she blushed so hard. I used to call her that when we were together. I knew I hit a spot with her because she was beaming harder.

"I'll check you later," I told her and walked out the door.

I could feel her standing in the doorway still staring at me. When I got into my car, I looked up and blew her a kiss. She closed the door right behind herself. I pulled off slowly and by the time I made it to the stop sign, Dreu was calling. *Damn I'm lucky;* I thought answering the phone.

"Hey Baby."

"Sup ma?"

"Just checking in."

"Yeah, you know what's up." I chuckled.

"Boy boo."

"Nah, what's up though? Can I come get you?"

"Umm..umm...not right now. My granny is calling me, I'll hit you back okay," she said and hung up.

I shook my head and sat my phone down. I was bored as fuck

with no plans. The traps were going smooth and everything was situated at the warehouse. I was really a boring ass nigga and it finally hit me.

Ring...Ring...Ring...

I looked down and grabbed my phone.

"Tell me something good"

"That spot on Naomi, that be slowing our paypa down and we put Pete on,"

"What about it?"

"That nigga Brick runs it."

"Is that right?" I rubbed my chin. This was music to my ears.

"Hell yeah. I'm sitting outside the crib right now."

"You see him?" I got hyped and sat up.

"Nah. I'm just sitting in the car. But the plate number I got, the whip right here."

"Aight good, good. Get that nigga and bring him to me East."

"I'll try nigga."

"Man, just snatch the nigga yo," I yelled upset.

This nigga know how bad I wanted this nigga. All this time I thought I had two niggas on my agenda, but God was making this shit easier for me. I was gonna kill two birds with one stone.

"I gotta go. The nigga coming out now," he said and hung up the phone. Because East was following him, I knew Brick wasn't at his spot. I bust a quick U-Turn and hopped on the 110 freeway back to the hood.

When I exited the freeway, I pulled into the Shell Gas Station on King and Figueroa. I pulled inside and jumped out heading inside to pay.

"Let me get $80 on 4," I told the attended then headed out.

I grabbed the two large gas cans I had and began feeling them up. I was hoping East was able to snatch the nigga before he came towards this way. I didn't need any distractions.

Pulling up to the spot, I watched the house to see if there was any movement. I sat there for an hour before a smoker had finally come. Because he stood in the door for a little over two minutes, I knew he was being served, which was good because whoever was in there was about to die a slow death. Making sure my strap was locked and loaded, I got out the car and crept around to the side of the house. Not wasting any time, I began drenching the house with the gasoline. I walked around the entire house making sure I emptied both cans. Satisfied with my work, I pulled out the matches and tossed them into the gasoline. In no time, the fire was growing rapidly. I headed back to the front and waited for the front to catch fire. Whoever was inside, hadn't even looked out the house.

What type of drug spot these niggas running; I thought shaking my head. These niggas was moving frivolous as fuck. Every last one of my spots had cameras surrounding them and that was protocol for any D Boy.

As the flames grew wild, I had to quickly move to get out the way.

"Anthony! Anthony!" I heard my name being called.

When I looked up the street, I saw a lady running my way with groceries in her hand. *How this bitch no my name?* I thought because she didn't look familiar. When she got close to me, she had so much worry in her eyes. She was crying hard and in a frantic.

"Dreu is in there!" she cried, hysterically.

"Dreu?" I asked puzzled.

"Yes Dee," she said again with tears now pouring like a broken faucet. I looked at the flames and they were now going into the house. My heart started beating faster, but I was stuck frozen. I was about to kill my baby.

To Be Continued!

Text Shan to 22828 to stay up to date with new releases, sneak peeks, contest, and more....

Subscribe

Text Shan to 22828 to stay up to date with new releases, sneak peeks, contest, and more....

Want to be a part of Shan Presents?

To submit your manuscript to Shan Presents, please send the first three chapters and synopsis to submissions@shanpresents.com

CPSIA information can be obtained
at www.ICGtesting.com
Printed in the USA
LVHW041626050219
606479LV00002B/291/P

9 781729 257326